"We're a pair," she said with a smile. "You're all bitter and gimpy, and I'm muddle-headed and weak as a kitten."

He laughed aloud, as if surprised by her blunt candor. "Bitter and gimpy, huh?" He pushed away from the tree trunk and patted the pistol he had tucked into a waistband holster attached to his jeans. "Well, that's where the Glock comes in handy. The great equalizer."

She eyed the gun, realizing for the first time that she'd allowed herself to go out in the woods alone with an armed stranger. Just how desperate had she become to find someone to trust?

Even now, with the possibility of treachery placed firmly in her head, she didn't feel afraid of Wade Cooper. Every instinct she had told her he was one of the good guys.

But could she really trust her instincts, with so much of her memory missing?

# PAULA GRAVES

# SECRET KEEPER

HARLEQUIN®
entertain, enrich, inspire™

For my fellow Intrigue authors,
who are a fine bunch of writers and an endless source
of encouragement, experience and support.

Recycling programs
for this product may
not exist in your area.

ISBN-13: 978-0-373-74693-4

SECRET KEEPER

Copyright © 2012 by Paula Graves

**Printed in U.S.A.**

## ABOUT THE AUTHOR

Alabama native Paula Graves wrote her first book, a mystery starring herself and her neighborhood friends, at the age of six. A voracious reader, Paula loves books that pair tantalizing mystery with compelling romance. When she's not reading or writing, she works as a creative director for a Birmingham advertising agency and spends time with her family and friends. She is a member of Southern Magic Romance Writers, Heart of Dixie Romance Writers and Romance Writers of America.

Paula invites readers to visit her website, www.paulagraves.com.

## Books by Paula Graves

# CAST OF CHARACTERS

*Annie Harlowe*—The D.C.-based reporter has no memory of the past three weeks of her life, or what happened to her parents, who had disappeared with her. Now Wade Cooper says she can trust him to keep her safe. But how can she trust anyone?

*Wade Cooper*—A war injury has left the former marine feeling like anything but a hero, but when a kidnapped woman escapes her captors and needs his help just to stay alive, can Wade rediscover his inner warrior?

*General Emmett Harlowe*—The air force general was one of three generals in charge of a dangerous peacekeeping mission in a war-plagued country in Central Asia. Are the national security secrets he possesses the reason for his recent abduction? Or does it have something to do with a mysterious coded journal?

*General Edward Ross*—The late army general kept a coded journal during his last few years of service. Now a whole lot of dangerous people want to get their hands on the journal. What secrets does it contain?

*Security Services Unit (SSU)*—MacLear Security's secret unit disbanded when the company fell to scandal. But many of the operatives are still working as mercenaries, with no moral code to guide them besides greed, making them extremely dangerous.

*Jesse Cooper*—Wade's brother is determined to figure out the secrets in the coded journal, certain the answer could help protect the country against dangerous forces aligned against it. But how far will he go, what will he risk, for the answers?

*Evie Marsh*—The daughter of U.S. Marine Corps general Baxter Marsh is convinced her father holds a key to the coded journal. But can she convince her stubborn parent to share what he knows with Cooper Security?

# Chapter One

Stars glittered across the vast wasteland spreading in front of her, blurred by the rain pouring down her face and into her eyes.

No, she thought, struggling for lucidity. Not stars. Couldn't be stars. Not on the ground.

Water. Must be water.

*Water. Water everywhere....*

A large, dark shape loomed ahead, slumbering in the downpour. *No lights there,* she thought bleakly. Just a hulking black nothing that should have been her salvation.

*Marsh.* The name came to her fuzzy brain, clawing for a foothold. *General Marsh.* Get General Marsh. General Marsh can help.

But General Marsh wasn't home.

She stumbled forward, coming to a stop only when she crashed sideways into the rough clapboard siding of the dark, silent house.

Maybe they were sleeping.

Her eyes drifted shut. Sleep. She needed sleep.

Some remnant of purpose slithered like a serpent deep inside her, jerking her back to unwanted consciousness. Her head throbbed in protest, but she pushed to her feet and weaved across the soggy ground to the front of the house.

The porch was wide but low slung, accessible by a couple of stumbling steps upward. She landed with a half tumble and caught herself on the old cane-bottomed rocker sitting by the front wall. Somehow avoiding an ungainly slump to the floor, she banged three times on the door. Cheek pressed against the solid wood, she listened for any sounds of movement from inside.

She heard nothing.

Tears burned her aching eyes, but she blinked them back, telling herself it was only the rain. Harlowes didn't cry.

She banged her hand against the door again with a sobbing gasp.

No answer.

She shoved away from the door, swaying toward the porch stairs. As she gripped the slick railing, the world seemed to twirl around her for a moment. Somehow, she made it safely to the bottom step.

But she didn't see the flagstone hidden in the rain-washed gloom.

Her toe caught the edge of the stone and she pitched forward. She tried to catch herself but her hand slipped on the wet grass and she hit hard, headfirst, on another flat stone.

Pain arced through her with a shower of bright sparkles. She pressed her hand to the side of her forehead and felt warm liquid mingling with the cold rain.

In the low light gleaming off the water, she saw rivulets of darkness spreading over her pale fingers. As she stared at the confusing sight, another drop of blackness splashed onto her palm. She had to wipe it off.

She dug her hands in the pockets of her jeans. The left side was empty, but in the right, she felt something thin and silky stuffed down into the bottom. She pulled it free and found herself holding a scarf.

It belonged to her mother. What was she doing with her mother's scarf?

She wiped her hand on it and pushed unsteadily to her feet, turning a full circle, taking in the unfamiliar world. There was water behind her. A house in front of her.

Why was she at the lake? Why was she standing in the rain?

A cottony sensation filled her head, as if the contents of her skull were too large to be contained. She shook her head and the world started to spiral around her again.

Okay. No more shaking her head. She started

toward the steps but stopped at the base, staring at the dark facade.

*Nobody's home,* she thought.

She wasn't sure how she knew it, but she did.

From somewhere not too far away came a noise. A car door, opening and closing. Footsteps crunching on a gravel drive. Even through the drumbeat of rain, the sound seemed clear and ominous.

Someone was near.

*Hide.*

She staggered away from the house, away from the lake. The woods thickened behind the lake house, rising toward the lowering clouds overhead. She was in the mountains.

An image of another house filled her mind. A sprawling pine cabin in the middle of the north Georgia mountains, where her parents were waiting.

She had to get there. They needed her.

Why did they need her?

Water slid into her eyes. She wiped it away, blinking at the blurry world around her. She had to get up the mountain.

Heading for the tree line, she stumbled as her feet caught in the underbrush. She caught herself on the trunk of a nearby pine, the rough bark scraping her palms, and somehow remained upright. But only for a few seconds. The next time the tangled vines of the forest floor ensnared her feet, she went down hard, landing on a bed of pine straw and mud.

She stared at the sideways world and saw only an alien landscape, full of mysteries and monsters. She closed her eyes, shutting everything out.

Slowly, blessedly, the world went away.

HE WASN'T GOING TO check the back door. The damned cat didn't belong to him. It was just a stray cat that hung around the house looking for scraps. Yeah, it came inside pretty regularly these days, but it had lived out in the rain for God knew how long before showing up on the back doorstep. The cat could surely handle a little September rainstorm.

Wade Cooper sank deeper in his recliner and tried to focus on the well-worn Dick Francis novel he'd been attempting to read for the past hour, ever since he got home from a long day at the office. But the moan of the wind in the trees outside conspired with the rattle of rain on his roof to draw his attention to the back door.

Ah, hell. It wouldn't hurt to take a quick look to see if the scruffy old tom was shivering on the back porch.

Rain blew in when he opened the door, a fine, cool mist reminding him fall had arrived, with winter just around the corner. A couple of years ago, Gossamer Ridge had seen near-record amounts of snowfall for an area that rarely saw the cold white stuff, and forecasters were hinting that another bad winter could be on the way.

Maybe he could coax the cat to stay inside more when the weather got cooler. Maybe feed him twice a day instead of once, and get him some toys to play with—

He stopped himself midthought.

*He's not your cat. He probably has a home and just mooches from everybody else in the area.*

Nobody else in the neighborhood had claimed him, but who would? The wiry tom was missing the tip of his left ear and he had extra toes on each foot. Plus, he ate like a horse and stole everything he could get his mouth around. Unfortunately, he'd decided that Wade deserved to be the recipient of his purloined bounty, which meant once a week, Wade took a basket full of the cat's haul around the neighborhood so people could reclaim the stolen socks, shoes, lawn tools and, on one humiliating occasion, a pair of women's thong underwear.

"Ernie?" he called to the darkness, peering through the rainy gloom.

There was no movement outside in response.

The hum of his cell phone vibrating on the coffee table gave him something else to think about. He shut out the rain and grabbed the phone. His brother Jesse's name stared back at him on the display. "Hey, Jesse."

"Just got in from Georgia. No luck." His brother

sounded tired. Cooper Security had recently joined the hunt for Air Force General Emmett Harlowe, his wife, Cathy, and their grown daughter, Annie, who'd disappeared almost three weeks earlier from their vacation cabin in the north Georgia mountains near Dahlonega. Jesse had spent the last three days in north Georgia, following up the dwindling leads.

"The Harlowes couldn't have disappeared into thin air." Wade sank into his chair again, grimacing at the twinge in his bum knee. "Their cabin wasn't that isolated, was it?"

"It's pretty far off the beaten track," Jesse admitted. "Nearest cabin is over a mile away. The last time anyone remembered seeing any of them was August nineteenth. That's several days before they were reported missing."

"No surveillance cameras in the area?" Wade asked.

"The police have checked every place in a fifty-mile radius."

"Have you tried talking to General Marsh again?"

Jesse's grim silence was an answer in itself. When he finally spoke, it was in a low growl. "He won't take my calls."

"Surely he'll take Evie's."

"I don't want to put her in the middle between the company and her father," Jesse said firmly. "I hired her for her accounting skills, not her relationship to Rita. And definitely not because of her father."

Wade thought his brother was being overly sensitive, given his tumultuous past relationship with Marsh's eldest daughter, Rita, but he knew better than to push him. Jesse had his own way of doing things, and arguing made him dig his heels in that much more firmly. "I could try calling him myself," he suggested.

"Do you think it would get you anywhere?"

Wade doubted it. He might not have the baggage of a failed engagement with Rita the way Jesse did, but it wasn't likely the general would talk to him, either. The family lived less than a quarter mile away, along the lakeshore, but they were hardly friendly neighbors.

Still, there were lives at stake, the missing Harlowes included. It was worth a try. "I won't know until I give it a go," he answered Jesse's question.

"Well, don't try it tonight," Jesse warned. "The general's one of those early to bed, early to rise types. And New York's an hour ahead."

"New York?"

"Oh, right. I didn't mention that. Evie said the general and his wife are in New York City with Rita. Trousseau shopping."

Ouch. "Rita's getting married?"

"Yeah. Some N.Y.U. professor she met when he was doing lectures at Emory. They hit it off and now she's gotten a job as a history lecturer at some high-priced private prep school in Manhattan."

Jesse hid it well, but Wade knew his brother still had some unhealed scars from his broken engagement to Rita Marsh, even though the relationship had ended years ago. Wade supposed Rita's upcoming marriage might make a few of those old scars bleed again.

Poor idiot.

"I'll email you the phone number. You can try him in the morning," Jesse said. "I've got to check with everyone else and see where we are on the rest of the caseload. Talk to you later."

Wade hung up and stared at his outstretched leg. It looked almost normal now, only the slightest bulge in the knee joint betraying the grievous injury that had nearly cost him his leg. Several surgeries and a knee replacement had spared him the fate of all too many of his fellow Marines. Though, considering how well some of his old military buddies were doing, artificial limbs and all, he had begun to wonder if the efforts to keep his leg had been a fool's errand.

The torn muscles, tendons and ligaments, along with some nerve damage, meant the leg would never be the same. He'd had to leave the Marines, unable to meet the fitness requirements anymore.

Jesse had taken him on at Cooper Security because he was a Cooper, not because there was much he could offer the company in his current state. He wasn't brainy like Isabel or cagey like Rick. He didn't have a special skill set like Shannon's computer genius or the analytical skills of his sister Megan. Before his injury, he'd been a bear of a man, strong and athletic, able to outrun and outfight anyone who challenged him.

All that was gone now.

*Stop feeling sorry for yourself.*

He pushed to his feet, ignoring the pain in his leg, and headed for the back door again. He might not be Super Marine anymore, but he could stop grousing about what he couldn't do and go get a poor, wet old tomcat out of the rain.

The rain had stopped while he was talking to Jesse, but a damp fog remained, curling around his neck like phantom fingers. He shook off a little shiver and called out the door. "Ernie!"

This time, at the sound of his voice, a gray apparition appeared out of the dark woods, streaking across the backyard and coming to a stop at the edge of the patio. Now sheltered by the metal awning, the cat took his time stalking across the concrete patio, his bushy gray tail twitching in the air.

He came with another gift, Wade saw with dismay. It looked like a red and gray scarf.

It was only when Ernie got closer that Wade saw red splotches on his pale gray muzzle, as well.

Ernie laid the gift at Wade's feet and purred softly.

Wade grimaced as he bent to pick up the scarf, his bum knee growling with pain. He let his good leg take most of his weight as he shook out the wet scarf. The drops of water that hit the patio at his feet were stained red.

Lifting the fabric to his nose, he sniffed. The metallic odor of blood hit him hard.

"Ernie, are you hurt?" Draping the scarf over the back of one of the outdoor chairs, he picked up the cat, even though he knew Ernie didn't like being handled. The cat wriggled but let him examine his red-stained muzzle without scratching or biting. The red came off easily, and Wade could see no sign of any injury to the cat.

But the blood seemed fresh. Had he caught a mouse or a squirrel before he committed his latest act of theft?

"Let's get inside, boy." He opened the door, and Ernie scooted inside. The cat waited patiently for him to pour food and settled in front of the water heater, munching the kibble from an old plastic bowl Wade had designated for the cat's use.

Wade went back outside and picked up the scarf. Taking another sniff, he caught a whiff of perfume mingled with the blood. The scarf itself was pale gray silk, more decorative than useful.

His gaze drawn to the woods from which Ernie

had emerged, Wade started limping across the yard to the edge of the tree line. "Hello?" he called into the dense darkness beyond.

There was no answer.

As he peered into woods, he felt something rub against his leg. Ernie had rejoined him, staring up at him with luminous green eyes. He must not have pulled the door completely closed.

"What did you find out there, boy?"

The cat sniffed the air and padded quietly into the woods. He went about five feet and stopped, looking back at Wade.

Was the bloody feline trying to lead him somewhere?

The cat continued forward. Wade followed.

The undergrowth grew more dense, vines and fallen limbs twisting around his ankles, making the trek into the woods unexpectedly perilous. For a man who'd grown up in these woods, who'd once considered them as much his home as the old brick and clapboard farmhouse where his father still lived, feeling alienated from his old playground was disconcerting.

It was the leg. The weakened muscles, the artificial joint, the constant sensation of feebleness—Wade felt as if he were dragging around an alien limb, one that could turn on him in an instant given the opportunity.

Panic rose like cold fingers up his spine. He

quelled the feeling with ruthless determination and upped his pace through the woods, ignoring the faint quiver low in his gut.

Ahead, Ernie had stopped near a broad-trunked oak tree. The cat moved cautiously around the tree, his tail flicking with curiosity. Wade caught up and circled the tree, as well.

The first thing he saw was a pale, blood-streaked hand. Small. Female.

Dark hair splayed out across the ground, wet from the rain and, in places, from blood, as well. Her face was half buried in the loamy mixture of old, dead leaves and newly fallen ones that carpeted the forest floor.

Wade started to kneel, grimacing at the sharp pain in his knee. He adjusted position, bending from the waist instead, and felt her throat for a pulse.

The woman moved at his touch, a quick, almost violent recoil. She turned wild, dark eyes toward him, though he didn't think she was actually seeing him. Blood coated one side of her face from a long gash near her hair line that was still oozing blood.

"I don't know anything," she gasped, slapping his hands away.

"Shh," Wade murmured, reaching into his pocket for his phone. "It's okay. You're going to be okay."

"I don't know…anything…." Her eyes rolled back in her head and she was out again. He punched

911 into the phone and checked her pulse again. Steady, if too fast. But her skin was icy to the touch. If she wasn't already going into shock, it wouldn't be long.

Wade shrugged off his jacket and laid it across her, tucking in the edges while he told the 911 dispatcher the situation. The injured woman made a low groaning sound, deep in her chest, but remained utterly still.

He couldn't make out much about her in the dark, other than a general description: female, young-ish, dark hair and dark eyes. There was something vaguely familiar about her, though he was pretty sure he'd never met her before.

The 911 dispatcher offered to stay on the line with him, but he told her he was going to call his cousin Aaron, a sheriff's deputy. He lived close by and might be able to beat the paramedics there.

Aaron answered on the second ring. "What's up, Wade?"

Wade explained what he'd stumbled onto. "Not sure what happened to her, but I think this could be a crime scene."

"On my way," Aaron said.

True to his word, Wade's cousin arrived within five minutes, ahead of the paramedics, swinging a bright flashlight as he moved toward Wade through the woods. "Wade?"

"Over here!" Wade waved him over.

Aaron hiked through the underbrush with ease, his long legs eating up big chunks of real estate at a time. He carried a large blanket in one arm and had his Smith & Wesson M&P 40 in his weapon hand. Behind him, his wife, Melissa, followed in his wake, struggling to keep up with her big husband's long strides.

Reaching Wade's side, Aaron aimed the flashlight beam toward the woman. Her eyelids crinkled when the bright light hit them, and she groaned again as she turned her face toward the ground to block out the light.

"That's a good sign, believe it or not," Melissa said, crouching beside the woman. She checked her carotid pulse, just as Wade had. "Ma'am? I need to take a look at you. Are you awake?"

Wade kicked himself. Why hadn't he been checking her over, trying to keep her awake? Had the damned Kaziri rebels shot all his good sense out of him when they nearly took off his knee?

*You can't crouch beside her. You can't kneel. Better to let someone able-bodied take over the hero business, right?*

"Wade?"

Wade looked up at his cousin, tamping down his irritation with his own weakness. "Yeah?"

"Take a look at her face." Aaron moved the beam of the flashlight over the woman's face again.

She had turned back toward them, some of the

blood on the side of her face smeared away by the leaves on the ground, revealing more of her features.

Wade's breath caught. "Son of a bitch."

"It's her, isn't it?" Aaron asked.

Wade nodded, gazing at the pale oval face of the woman he and his family had spent the last three weeks trying to find.

Melissa looked up at them. "Who?"

"Annie Harlowe," Wade answered. Daughter of the missing Air Force general.

Aaron looked at Wade, his expression grim. "So if she's here, where the hell's the general?"

## Chapter Two

Annie couldn't remember the dream, only that it had left her heart thundering in her chest and her stomach roiling with nausea. She woke to pain—in her shoulders, her wrists, her knees and especially her head, which felt as if it had been hollowed out and filled with burning agony.

For some reason, she expected to open her eyes to bright lights and chaos, but the room around her was blessedly dark, save for a faint light seeping in from the doorway several feet away. The unfamiliar bed supporting her weakened body was uncomfortable, the gloom-shrouded surroundings dull and sterile.

A shadow moved to her right, and her heart skipped a beat.

"You're awake." The voice was low and soft, broadened by a southern accent.

"Who are you? Where am I?"

"I'm Wade Cooper," the shadow answered. "And

you're on the fourth floor of Chickasaw County Hospital."

The pain made a little more sense. "How'd I get here?"

"I found you semiconscious in the woods near Gossamer Lake."

She narrowed her eyes and instantly regretted it as agony streaked through her forehead. She lifted her hand to the aching spot and found a bandage. "What happened to me?"

"Don't know yet," Wade said. "Think you can handle the light?"

She wanted to say no, as she was pretty sure the last thing her throbbing brain could handle was anything bright. But she didn't like talking to a shadow, so she said, "Yes."

He rose to his feet and turned on a light over the bed. After the initial shock, her eyes adjusted quickly to the mercifully dim light and the headache settled into bearable territory. Her visitor sat down, giving her a better look at him. Early thirties, she guessed. Lean and fit, with broad shoulders and a pugnaciously masculine jaw. In the low light, his eyes looked coal-black and mysterious, but his calm, neutral expression suggested her mind was playing tricks on her.

"You okay?" he asked.

"I think so." She noted his clothing—jeans and

a green plaid shirt under a faded denim jacket. "You're not a doctor."

He smiled, flashing a set of straight white teeth. "No ma'am, I'm not."

"Where did you say I am, Chickasaw County? In Georgia?" She couldn't remember if there was a Chickasaw County in Georgia. She seemed to have a lot of gaps in her memory all of a sudden.

"Chickasaw County, Alabama," he corrected.

"Alabama?" She frowned, the movement sending another dart of pain through her injured scalp. What the hell was she doing in Alabama?

"You don't remember how you got here?"

Before she could answer the question, the door to the hospital room opened and a man in green surgical scrubs entered, holding a chart. His eyes widened with surprise when they met hers. "You're awake." He glanced at Wade. "And you have a visitor," he added, his tone disapproving. "Well past visiting hours."

Wade looked briefly sheepish but didn't move. "I didn't want her to wake up in the hospital all alone."

Annie slanted a quick look at him, surprised by the kindness in his voice. She worked in Washington, D.C., where random acts of kindness weren't exactly the norm, at least not in the circles in which she ran.

"Nice of you," the doctor said without much sincerity in his clipped tone. "But I need to examine my patient now."

Wade started moving toward the door. For the first time, Annie saw that he walked with a visible limp.

"Wait," she said as he reached the exit.

He turned in the doorway, his powerful shoulders and lean hips silhouetted by the light from the corridor. Built like a cowboy, she thought, her dry lips curving at the notion. "Yeah?" he said.

"Are you leaving? The hospital, I mean." Hating the neediness she heard in her voice, she told herself she'd be better off if he said yes.

"No, I reckon I'll stick around a bit." His face was in shadow, but she thought she could make out a smile.

Then he was gone, leaving her alone with the doctor.

"I didn't get your name," she said to the doctor.

"Dr. Brady Ambrose," he answered briskly, reaching for her wrist to check her pulse. Even the skin of her wrists hurt when he touched them. "How long have you been awake?"

"I don't know—a few minutes?"

He checked her eyes with a pen light. "Headache?"

"Oh, yeah."

"Anything else hurt?"

"Everything else hurts," she admitted. New aches and pains seemed to be cropping up with each passing second. She looked at her wrist, which still stung from the doctor's touch, and saw a deep purplish-red bracelet of bruises and abrasions. She lifted her other hand and found the same marks.

Those were ligature marks, she realized with rising alarm.

"What day is it?" she asked.

"Friday." The doctor looked at his watch. "Actually, Saturday by now," he added with a rueful smile.

"The date, I mean."

"September 8."

Her alarm exploded into full blown panic. "September?" That wasn't possible. Just this morning, she'd flown from D.C. to Chattanooga to meet her parents at the airport for the drive to their vacation cabin north of Dahlonega. The last thing she remembered was—

What? What was the last thing she remembered?

Nothing. The airport was the last thing she remembered. Walking through the terminal, grabbing her suitcase from the baggage carousel and heading off to look for her parents, who would be waiting to pick her up.

That had been August 18.

Almost three weeks of her life were missing.

"She seems lucid," Wade told his brother Jesse, who sat across from him in the fourth floor waiting room. "But I don't think she remembers what happened to her and her parents. It would have been the first thing she'd have asked about, don't you think?"

Jesse ran his palm across his face, his eyes dark with frustration. "So it's not going to be the lead we hoped."

Next to him, their sister Megan shot Jesse a sharp look. "A woman I was pretty sure had to be dead turned out to be alive," she said flatly. "That's not nothing."

"Of course not," Jesse agreed with a faint smile. "But we aren't any closer to decoding General Ross's journal than we were before."

"Maybe she doesn't remember now," Megan said, "but that doesn't mean she won't remember eventually. Remember when Hannah was attacked and lost some of her memories? They eventually came back."

"Eventually," Jesse agreed. "But three weeks have already passed. And apparently she escaped from her captors, which may put her parents in even graver danger."

"She's not out of danger, either." Wade looked toward the waiting room door, remembering the look of confusion and vulnerability in Annie Harlowe's caramel-brown eyes. "If she escaped, she may know something that could lead us to the kidnappers. And they'll be looking to stop her from telling what she knows."

"The kidnappers won't be the only people who'll want custody of her," Jesse warned. "I imagine the Pentagon will want to know everything she knows about what happened to her father, too."

Wade nodded. The Department of Defense certainly wasn't feeling very sanguine about a recently retired Air Force general with years of operational secrets stored in his brain going missing for three weeks. The hunt for the missing general was all over the news, with conspiracy theories flying all over twenty-four-hour cable news channels.

Coverage of his missing wife and daughter had been tangential in comparison, thanks to the general's potential significance to American national security. But the news shows had flashed their photos often enough. Someone in the hospital could have already recognized Annie Harlowe's name and face.

Wade stood and limped over to the window, which looked down on the front entrance of the hospital four stories below. No news trucks yet. But information would get out soon enough. Then what?

"We have a limited window of opportunity to get anything out of her," he told Jesse, who'd crossed to stand next to him at the window.

"Aaron's supposed to be here any minute to ask her questions in an official capacity."

Aaron had called in a crew of Chickasaw County deputies to do a grid search of the woods behind Wade's house. Along with his wife, Melissa, he'd stayed with them to direct the search while Wade followed the ambulance to the hospital.

"That may not be soon enough," Wade warned, spotting a Huntsville television news van moving up the drive toward the hospital entrance.

Megan joined them at the window. "Here come the newsboys," she said with a grimace.

"They're just doing their job," Jesse said.

"They'll be all over her like stink on a pig."

Wade had to smile at his sister's description. Apt, probably, but Jesse was right. The news people had a job to do.

Just like he did.

"I'm going to go see if the doctor is finished examining her," he told his brother and sister. "Why don't y'all go see if you can waylay the reporters for a little while?"

Jesse clapped him on his shoulder. "What are you going to tell her?"

"The truth," Wade answered simply.

The door to Annie Harlowe's hospital room was half open when he reached it. He listened for the doctor's voice but heard only a soft, snuffling sound coming from within the room.

Crying, he thought, his heart twisting with a disconcerting mixture of sympathy and dread.

He made himself knock lightly on the door. "Annie, it's Wade Cooper. Can I come in?"

There was a long pause before she answered. "Yes."

He crossed to her bed, trying to keep his limp to a minimum. He wasn't very successful. She lay with her head turned away from him, as if she were staring out the window. But the window shades were drawn.

"What did the doctor have to say?"

"I have a concussion. Some scrapes and contusions." She turned her face toward him. Her eyes were red-rimmed but dry. "And I'm missing three weeks of my life."

INTERESTING, ANNIE THOUGHT, watching Wade Cooper's face for a response. His only reaction was a softening in his dark eyes, a hint of sympathy creasing his forehead.

Her words came as no surprise to him.

"You already know who I am," she whispered.

Wade sat in the chair by her bed. "You've been all over the news for three weeks."

"Why aren't my parents here? Has anybody even thought to call them?" They must be frantic, she thought, showing up at the airport only to discover their daughter had disappeared from the airport without a trace.

Or had there been a trace? She didn't know. Everything after the baggage carousel was a big blank.

"What's the last thing you remember?" Wade asked.

"Arriving at the Chattanooga airport," she answered, not liking the fact that he hadn't answered her question. "Where are my parents?"

"We don't know," Wade said. "You all went missing at the same time."

She stared at him, nausea rising in her gut. "My parents are missing?"

"You don't remember anything after the airport?"

"No. I thought—I assumed that's where I was abducted or whatever." A new, horrifying thought blackened her mind. "Was I—did anybody check to see if I was raped?"

Wade's face blanched. "I don't know."

She struggled against a sudden flood of nausea. "I think I'm going to be sick."

Wade grabbed a small bedpan from the table by the bed and thrust it into her hands. A series of dry heaves racked her aching body, but apparently her stomach was empty, for nothing came up.

Wade disappeared from view for a moment, returning with a wet washcloth from the bathroom.

He handed it to her and she took it gratefully, pressing the cool cloth against her mouth.

"I know they looked you over carefully in the E.R. before they brought you to a room," Wade said gently. "There was a female deputy with you, so they probably checked for that. I think the doctor would have told you if they'd found anything."

"Three weeks," she rasped, her throat aching. "They might not even find anything after three weeks—"

Wade closed his hand over hers. Heat spread through her from his warm, firm touch, helping to settle the shakes that threatened to take over her body. She took a couple of deep breaths, willing herself to deal with what she knew rather than what she didn't.

She had to separate herself from how the story affected her personally and stick with the facts. She had to think like a reporter.

"Is there a theory behind what happened to me and my parents?" she asked aloud, dreading what Wade's answer might be.

He hesitated before he spoke, drawing her gaze to his eyes to see whether she'd find truth in them or more secrets. "The official story is that the investigators have formed no theories."

"And unofficially?"

"The fact that your father is such a high-ranking military officer suggests a national security angle."

Of course, if she were thinking straight, the thought would have crossed her mind already.

And there was also her father's odd behavior when he'd called her the Monday before her flight to Chattanooga to ask her to make time for a family vacation the next week. "There's something I need to tell you about," he'd said, sounding serious.

Had he ever gotten a chance to tell her whatever he'd wanted to share?

"How did anyone kidnap all three of us from a busy airport?" she wondered aloud.

"They didn't," Wade answered, squeezing her arm with gentle strength. She looked down at his long fingers, at the play of muscles and tendons in the back of his lean hand as he squeezed again and let go. "You and your parents arrived at the cabin on the eighteenth of August as planned. The caretaker handed the key over to your father, and you and your mother were both there with him. You were seen the next morning in Dahlonega, where you'd apparently gone for breakfast. The caretaker remembered seeing you and your parents return in your father's silver Ford Expedition around ten-thirty on the nineteenth. That's the last anyone saw of you."

She shook her head. "I don't remember any of that."

"Your concussion could have caused a memory loss."

"Will I get it back?"

"I don't know."

The nausea was knocking on the back of her throat again. She wrestled it back to mere queasiness. "Why do I get the feeling you know more about what happened to me than I do?"

"I don't think I do."

He sounded honest enough, but she saw more mysteries behind those big brown eyes. "You're keeping something from me."

Wade Cooper was saved by a knock on the door. When nobody entered a moment later, Wade stood. "I'll see who it is."

He crossed to the door, favoring his right leg. His right knee looked a little larger than his left, straining against the faded jeans he wore. Bum knee?

He spoke in low tones to someone outside the door. The other voice sounded male as well, but she couldn't make out what he was saying. Wade closed the door behind him and returned to her side, pulling his chair closer. His dark eyes were deadly serious.

"Two men from the Air Force Office of Special Investigations are downstairs asking to talk to you. It's up to you. If you want to talk to them, fine. If you want to wait until you're feeling better, that's fine, too."

The last thing she wanted to do was face an interrogation by the A.F.O.S.I. But all she'd be doing was putting off the inevitable. "You can tell them I'll see them."

Wade nodded and stood. Reaching into his pocket, he drew out a narrow wallet. He removed a card from one of the inside pockets and handed it to her. "That has my cell number on it. You need to talk to me about anything, you call. Understand?"

His urgent tone made her stomach hurt, but she nodded, wincing at the flare of pain in her head. "Are you leaving?"

He shook his head. "I'll be just down the hall. Call that number, and I'll come running."

As he disappeared through the doorway, she released a slow, shaky breath. She wasn't used to feeling weak and vulnerable. She hated it. But her world had upended in the span of a few minutes—or, more accurately, three missing weeks. She had to find her feet again.

She had to find out what happened to her parents.

A brief knock on the door preceded two men dressed in dark suits who entered the room in tandem. They filled the small space with an air of authority, introducing themselves as Braddock and Hartman from the A.F.O.S.I. Braddock, who was taller, darker and leaner than stocky, sandy-haired Hartman, did most of the talking. Hartman stood slightly behind the other man, holding a small duffel bag. Annie eyed the bag with curiosity.

"We need to know everything you can tell us

about the incident in Georgia," he began without further preamble.

"I can't tell you anything," she said carefully. "I have a head injury and I don't remember any of it."

Braddock's eyebrows inched upward. "Nothing?"

"Nothing."

The two men exchanged a look that gave her the creeps.

"Could I see your identification?" she asked.

Their gazes snapped to her. Braddock's tense expression melted into an engaging smile. "Certainly." He reached into the breast pocket of his suit jacket.

Annie tensed, an image flashing through her muddled brain. A needle, glistening in the glow of a single, bare bulb. A tiny droplet of moisture trembling on the point before it fell.

Panic seized her insides, threatening to turn them to liquid.

The man withdrew his hand. It held only a flat black wallet. He flipped it open and showed her an official-looking name badge. Arthur Braddock with the Air Force Office of Special Investigations. Looked legit.

So why couldn't she shake the feeling these guys were anything but what they claimed to be?

"What is the last thing you remember before waking up?"

"I was standing at the luggage carousel at the Chattanooga airport," she answered.

"And you remember nothing else?" Braddock sounded skeptical.

"I have vague memories of being in the emergency room earlier tonight, I think," she answered carefully. She didn't mention the image of the needle, mostly because she didn't really trust these two men. But the truth was, she did have some memories of being examined in the emergency room. They'd cut off her clothes. Poked and prodded and X-rayed. She had a vague memory of being in a cool, white cavern—a CAT scanner?

"Why were you and your parents in Georgia?"

"Vacation. We like to get together once or twice a year."

"Just the three of you?"

"We had plans for lunch with my aunt Phyllis on Thursday." Her mother's sister lived in Gainesville, Georgia. They usually tried to meet her for lunch or dinner at least once during each trip. Annie guessed they hadn't made it to lunch, if the last time she and her parents had been seen was on the nineteenth.

"Your aunt is the one who reported you missing," Hartman said.

Braddock looked at the other man. Annie got the feeling he'd prefer that Hartman stay quiet.

"I really don't have anything else I can add," Annie said.

"I think you probably know more than you realize. We'd like to take you back to Quantico with us. There's a hospital on base that can see to your medical needs, and the staff psychiatrists can help you work on recovering more of your missing memories." Braddock's voice was gentle and encouraging, but Annie realized, with alarm, that she didn't believe a bit of it.

These people were not here to help her.

"We'll need you to sign the transfer papers for the hospital, so they'll release you. We can transport you tonight."

*Don't go with them. Whatever you do, don't let these men get you alone.* The voice she heard in her head wasn't her own. It was her father's, the low, gravelly coastal Carolina drawl she'd always loved so much.

"I don't have any clothes—they cut them off of me in the E.R."

"We've brought you some clothes to wear." Hartman put the duffel bag on the bottom of her bed and stepped back.

"You thought of everything," Annie murmured. She faked a smile. "Okay, then. I need a few minutes alone to get dressed," she said quietly. "That will give you time to finalize the transfer with the hospital staff. Then I'll sign the papers, and we can go."

Braddock and Hartman exchanged glances. "Okay," Braddock said with what she supposed was meant to be a gentle smile. The expression looked predatory.

To her relief, they left the room, closing the door behind them. She slumped back against her pillows, her pulse pounding a cadence of agony in her head. With shaking hand, she reached for the phone on the small bedside table and pulled it onto the bed next to her.

Opening her hand, she looked at the slightly rumpled card she'd held in her tightly clutched fist during the meeting with Braddock and Hartman.

*Wade Cooper. Cooper Security.*

She picked up the receiver and dialed the number.

Wade Cooper answered on the first ring. "Cooper."

"They want to transfer me to a hospital in Quantico," she said without preamble, keeping her voice low, in case the men were just outside the room, listening in.

"Do you think that's a good idea?" he asked.

"No," she answered flatly. "I think you need to get me out of this hospital. Right now."

## Chapter Three

Two men in dark suits flanked the door to Annie Harlowe's room. Annie had said they'd told her they were going to coordinate the release papers with the hospital, but Wade had a feeling they already had plans for how to remove her from the hospital without going through any channels. If she was right—if these men were imposters—the last thing they'd want to do was deal with hospital red tape.

What he needed was a distraction.

He slipped back inside the waiting room. "Two men guarding her door. Possibly armed—can't tell from a look."

Aaron and Melissa had joined the three of them, arriving just as Annie was calling Wade. He felt a hint of relief at having his younger cousin around for whatever came next. His position as a deputy, not to mention the Smith & Wesson M&P 40 he wore in a belt holster beneath his green Chickasaw County Sheriff's Department jackets, added a heartening amount of heft to their makeshift rescue operation.

"We need a distraction," Megan said.

Jesse had been across the room on the phone. He returned, his expression grim. "They're not A.F.O.S.I. Mason Hunter just checked with a friend of his who's been working this case for the Air Force." Hunter was a fellow Cooper Security operative who had once been an Air Force major. "Nobody there has heard anything about finding Annie Harlowe."

Wade grimaced. "Until now."

Jesse shook his head. "Mason was discreet. Treated it like a routine touching-base thing."

"So like I said," Megan said, "we need a distraction."

"I can get security to take them off for questioning," Aaron suggested.

"They'll flash badges and tell security to stand down," Jesse disagreed.

"Or say to hell with the charade and start shooting," Wade countered.

"If they're not A.F.O.S.I., who are they?" Megan asked.

"Do you really have to ask?" Aaron growled.

"S.S.U." Wade grimaced.

"We have to assume it's them," Jesse agreed.

Wade wished he could believe otherwise, but bitter experience told him there were few other possibilities. The collapse of MacLear Security, once one of the top private security contractors in the world, should have been the end of the company's Special Services Unit—the S.S.U. It had been the illegal actions of that secret army of ruthless, corrupt mercenaries that had brought down the once well-respected, legitimate security company.

But some of the S.S.U. had avoided indictments and joined forces as a band of guns for hire. Cooper Security had come across the S.S.U. several times in recent months, each encounter more alarming than the last. Left to their own devices, without the need to maintain an air of legitimacy, the S.S.U. agents had become bolder and more ruthless than ever.

"We're certain the S.S.U. was involved in the abduction of the Harlowes, aren't we?" Megan asked.

"As sure as we can be without hard evidence," Jesse agreed.

"They were trained by former feds at MacLear," Megan said, "so they certainly would know how to pass themselves off as federal agents."

Meanwhile, Wade thought, the clock was ticking. He had to get Annie Harlowe out of that hospital room without those two men in suits catching him. But what would coax them away from the door?

He pulled out his cell phone and dialed the last number, Annie's hospital room. She answered on the second ring, her voice cautious.

"Braddock and Hartman are standing right outside your room," Wade told her. "We need them to go somewhere else for a while. Here's what I want you to do." He outlined a plan he hoped would work.

She was silent a moment, then said, "Okay. Let's do it."

Wade hung up the phone and turned to his sister, who gazed up at him with a grin. "I'll go find some scrubs," she said.

THE MINUTE SHE'D HUNG UP the phone with Wade Cooper, Annie began to second-guess herself. What made her think the stranger who'd found her in the woods was any less dangerous than the two men who'd just left her hospital room? He had secretive eyes, and unlike the man who'd just flashed his badge at her, Wade hadn't shown her anything but a slightly rumpled business card. Anyone could print up business cards.

She looked down at the card: Cooper Security. The name sounded familiar. Something to do with a recently indicted former State Department official named Barton Reid. Someone at Cooper Security had been involved with gathering evidence against him, right?

She pressed her fingertips against her forehead, wishing her head would stop hurting. Her pulse pounded like a jackhammer in her ears. She couldn't imagine all this stress could be good for her concussed condition.

*One thing at a time, Annie.* First order of business—get dressed. Over the phone Wade had told her he'd brought her a change of clothes, borrowed from his sister, for when she was released. She needed to put them on now so they could leave the hospital without anyone asking questions.

She had to remove the IV in the back of her hand in order to move at all. With a wince at the biting pain, she removed the cannula and pressed her fingertip against the open vein to stanch the bleeding. Though a little dizzy, she managed to keep her balance long enough to reach the small in-room closet and pull out the bag Wade had told her would be at the bottom.

Inside the bag, she found a pair of sweat pants and a long-sleeved thermal T-shirt. The loose-fitting clothes nearly swallowed her whole, though they were actually a size smaller than she normally wore. She must have lost weight sometime over the last three weeks.

Had her captors starved her? Was that the least of the things they'd done to her?

*Don't think about it. Just get dressed and get ready.*

She'd just pushed her feet into the slip-on sneakers she'd found at the bottom of the bag when she heard voices outside her room. She scurried back to her bed, nearly stumbling on the way, and pulled the covers over her to hide her clothing.

A red-haired nurse in blue scrubs entered her room, carrying a bottle of juice. She gave Annie a quick smile and handed over the juice. "I'll take your friends down to the clerk's office so they can get our doctor to sign off on the transfer," she said brightly. She had a broad rural drawl, intelligent gray eyes and a quirky smile. "I'm Megan Pike," she told Annie in a lower voice. "Wade's sister."

Wade had told Annie that he was sending his sister in, but Annie couldn't see much resemblance between this fair-skinned, freckled woman and her dark-haired brother with his olive skin and mysterious midnight eyes.

"What happens next?"

"My cousin Aaron is down the hall within sight. If the men don't come with me willingly, he'll confront them and, if necessary, take them into custody." Megan smiled briefly. "He's a deputy. And big as the side of a barn."

"I'm not sure those men aren't armed," Annie warned.

"Neither are we, but Aaron and my brothers are all armed. I don't think anyone wants a shootout in a hospital, including those guys outside." Megan tried to sound confident, but she couldn't quite sell it.

"Do you know who they are?"

"We think we do," Megan admitted. "Wade will explain everything as soon as we get you to a safe place."

"Which is where?"

"Wade's place, for now." Megan glanced over her shoulder. "I've got to get this show on the road. Just wait right here. If you hear trouble starting, get behind your bed and take cover."

Annie's chest tightened with alarm. "You think that could happen, don't you?"

"I don't know," Megan admitted. She went outside. Annie heard more voices. One of the men raised his voice enough for her to hear him say, "Is that really necessary?"

"It is," Megan said firmly. "It will only take a couple of minutes."

Finally, footsteps moved away from her door. Annie eased herself into an upright position on the bed, her gaze glued to the door.

A minute later, the door swung open. Annie held her breath.

Wade Cooper's cowboy silhouette filled the doorway. He was holding the handles of a wheelchair. "Time to hit the road," he said softly, rolling the chair over to the bed.

"Maybe I'm overreacting. Maybe those people are who they say they are and I'm just looking for dragons to fight—"

"They're not." He motioned for her to get into the chair.

"I don't think I need a wheelchair."

"It will look more natural, at least until we reach the tunnel."

"The tunnel?"

"There's a tunnel from the basement floor that leads out to the parking deck." He held out his hand to help her into the chair.

She took his hand, somehow calmed by the heat of his strong, firm touch. When she settled into the chair, he let go, leaving her fingers tingling and cold. "Then what?"

"We'll wheel you down the tunnel, and then leave the chair there. Jesse's gone to drive the car around to the exit. We'll whisk you out of here and I'll take you to my place until we can figure out what to do next."

She wished he sounded more confident, but she could hear the thread of uncertainty running through his deep, calm voice. She had a lot of questions for him, since she was certain Wade Cooper knew more about her parents' abduction than she did at this point.

But the first order of business was to get safely out of the hospital.

There were two other passengers on the fourth floor elevator when the doors opened. Annie smiled at them briefly, making a quick assessment. One was clearly a phlebotomist, carrying a rectangular plastic basket full of vials, bandages, rubber tourniquets and other blood-taking paraphernalia. The other was a haggard-looking man in his fifties in rumpled clothes who didn't seem to have the energy to return the smile.

The phlebotomist got off on the fourth floor. The haggard-looking man stayed with them.

The elevator stopped at each floor, taking on new passengers. A woman with red-rimmed eyes. A man with a clerical collar who smiled back gently at Annie when he entered. A man holding a sleeping child tucked against his shoulder. Annie tried not to look at them all as potential dangers, but she couldn't seem to stop herself.

She'd seen too much of life as a reporter to believe that all people were good. They weren't. Many of them were, maybe even most of them, but there were enough bad actors to make the world a perilous place.

The elevator emptied at the lobby floor. Wade wheeled her out as well, taking a quick circuit around the lobby with her until their fellow passengers had all left through the front door.

Wade circled her back to the elevators and pushed her chair to a different elevator. He pushed the down button and the doors swished open. This elevator was narrower, not set up to accommodate the big, wide gurneys that the other cars were built to handle.

Wade wheeled her inside and hit the button for the basement on the panel.

"You engage in this kind of subterfuge often?" she asked with a wry half smile. Her voice seemed loud in the empty car.

"Not too often," he answered. For a brief second, his big, warm hand settled on her shoulder. The touch had an electric effect on her nervous system, shooting sparks that lingered even after he removed his hand.

"Do you live far away?"

"About ten minutes from here. We'll be there before you know it."

"What if it's not safe for me to leave the hospital?" she asked. "Medically, I mean." After all, concussions weren't anything to mess around with. The doctor had said he'd want to keep her another day, maybe two, just to be sure the brain injury wasn't any more serious.

"We've already called the Cooper Security doctor on staff. If he thinks you need round-the-clock care, he'll arrange it."

"Just not in a public hospital?" she guessed.

"Right."

"Cooper Security," she repeated, the name once again niggling at the back of her scrambled brains.

"You had something to do with Barton Reid's most recent indictment, right?"

"Tangentially," Wade agreed. The elevator hit the basement floor and dinged, the doors swishing open. He wheeled her out into a well-lit but featureless corridor.

The dingy white walls of the long tunnel were unadorned, save for security cameras spaced every twenty yards or so. "They'll be able to see how I left," she murmured.

"Won't matter," he said.

"Why not?"

"Because you're not doing anything illegal, and my cousin is currently informing the hospital security staff that you're being removed from the hospital under authority of the Chickasaw County Sheriff's Department."

"He can do that?"

"The sheriff can, and Aaron's arranged it with him."

"Won't the sheriff want to know where I am?"

"Sheriff Canaday has an understanding with Cooper Security. We deal with a lot of high-risk security cases."

"The real A.F.O.S.I. is going to want to talk to me," she warned.

"I imagine the FBI will, too," Wade affirmed as they passed the final security camera in the tunnel. "I have a cousin in the Huntsville Resident

Agency—we'll call him in a few days and see how they want to proceed."

Annie's head was starting to swim. "I feel as if I've awakened in the middle of a spy movie."

Wade laughed softly, the warm, rich sound catching her by surprise. "Believe it or not, I know what you mean."

The wheels of the wheelchair rattling on the dull tile flooring made a loud clatter that echoed off the walls of the tunnel, drowning out almost everything else. But not even the squeaky wheels could mask the loud ding of the elevator at the other end of the hall.

"Is that—?"

Wade paused a second, then suddenly started running. She felt his breath hot in her ear as they picked up speed and heard, when his steps quickened, that his limp nearly disappeared when he ran. Behind them, the pounding of footsteps on the linoleum echoed down the tunnel.

"Wade—"

"Almost there," he breathed, his shoes squeaking on the floor. He sounded almost as scared as she felt.

The chair made it impossible for her to turn around and look to see who was coming behind them. But who else could it be? The men who'd come to her room to take her away had apparently figured out where she'd gone.

They reached the end of the long tunnel, where a heavy-looking steel door stood between them and whatever came next. Through the large square window set into the door, Annie glimpsed a concrete parking deck before Wade hurried around the chair and held out his hands. "We have to run," he urged, his dark eyes meeting hers.

She let him pull her to her feet, daring a quick look behind them as they ran for the door. The two fake A.F.O.S.I. agents were gaining on them, only fifty yards back down the tunnel.

Wade pushed open the door and pulled her outside with him, emerging into a dimly lit parking garage at a sprint.

But there was no getaway vehicle waiting for them.

## Chapter Four

Next to Annie, Wade Cooper breathed a low, heartfelt profanity.

She looked over her shoulder at the window in the tunnel doorway, panic clawing at her gut. Only twenty yards away now, the two men in black suits raced for the door right behind them.

A squeal of tires drew her attention back to the parking deck. She saw Wade waving wildly at a large black Ford Expedition coming toward them at a clip. It braked to a quick stop and the back door opened. Annie caught a glimpse of Megan Pike's pale, freckled face as Wade pushed her into the backseat and clambered in behind her.

"Go!" he commanded the man in the driver's seat. All Annie could see of him was a head of dark hair and, in the rearview mirror, a pair of dark eyes even more mysterious than Wade Cooper's.

Wade twisted around to look behind them. Annie turned, too, ignoring the wave of dizziness caused by the rapid movement of her head, and spotted their pursuers bursting through the tunnel door just as the Expedition descended the wide curve of the parking deck, putting the men out of sight.

Annie turned back around, slumping against the seat. Her nausea had returned with a vengeance, but she fought it, closing her eyes.

She felt Wade's hand close over hers. "You okay?"

"Just feeling a little queasy."

"Here." From her left, Megan thrust a plastic sack into her hands.

"No, I'm okay," Annie assured her breathlessly. "I just need to breathe."

"We can open a window," Megan suggested.

"Not a good idea," the man in the front seat suggested.

"The windows are bullet-resistant," Wade said quietly.

"Who *are* you people?" Annie opened her eyes to look at Wade.

"We're people who are almost as invested as you are in what happened to your parents," the driver answered.

*How was that possible?*

"I know you have questions," Wade said quietly. His fingers tightened over hers. "And we'll answer them all. I promise. Just let us get you to a safe place and have the doctor take a look at you, okay?"

She wanted to trust him, she realized. She needed

to. She was hurt and tired, terrified about what may have happened to her parents and scared for her own safety. She'd never felt more alone in her life.

But how could she trust any of them? How had she allowed herself to become so utterly in their control without even asking any hard questions?

Her head felt like lead. She felt as if her neck could barely hold it up. Even the effort of keeping her eyes open seemed beyond her ability at the moment. If she had to fight her way out of their clutches, she wouldn't be able to do it. So she had no choice but to trust them, to go along with them, at least for the moment, hoping she was right to put her life in their hands.

But as soon as she got even a drop of her strength back, she'd have a hell of a lot of hard questions for Wade Cooper and his family.

"Is she unconscious?" That was Megan Pike's voice. It drifted through the cottony haze that had set up shop in her brain, nudging her to consciousness again. She forced open her heavy eyes and saw that the SUV had stopped, the engine noise dying away.

"I'm awake," she murmured. Her voice came out thick and slurred. She forced herself into a more upright position, her whole body feeling like a bad toothache. Every muscle cramped, every ligament and tendon complained. The nausea was back and she dry heaved a couple of times into the plastic bag Megan had given her.

"Okay, time to see a doctor," Wade said firmly, his hand warm against the back of her neck.

"Just give me a minute," she gasped.

"I'll call Eric and see what's holding him up," Megan said. She climbed out of the car, shutting the door behind her. The driver got out as well, leaving Annie alone in the backseat with Wade.

"I know you're probably scared," he said in a low, soothing growl. "I don't blame you. I'd be pretty scared, too."

She rubbed her burning eyes. "I keep thinking I'm going to wake up and the world will make sense again."

"We'll see what we can do about helping it make sense again."

The nausea subsided enough that she was able to raise her head and look up at him. Up close, his dark eyes looked warm and gentle, no hint of the earlier mystery. She felt as if she could drown in those eyes. It was an oddly comforting feeling, even though there was a part of her foggy brain that was clanging with warning bells.

*Don't depend on anyone else. Don't trust anyone else.*

*Never, ever get involved.*

"Where are we?" She forced herself to look away from those liquid brown eyes and take in the world outside the SUV. They were parked in front of a cabin surrounded by tall pines and hardwoods. In front of them, beyond a long carpet of fallen pine straw, moonlight sparkled on the calm, mirrored surface of a lake.

An image filled her mind. A field of stars stretching out in front of her, twinkling and shimmering as she walked toward their light.

Not stars. Lights on water.

She'd been here before.

"I was here," she murmured.

"Not here," Wade disagreed, sliding out of the SUV and turning to face her. "But not far away."

He held out his hand. She took it and eased her aching body out of the car. The September night was cooler than she'd expected, and she couldn't hold back a shiver.

"Let's get you inside where it's warm," Wade murmured, wrapping his arm around her shoulders and tucking her close. Any other time, she might have taken offense at a strange man being so presumptuous as to touch her that way, but frankly, she was glad for the warmth and the solid heft of him, holding her upright as they carefully walked the uneven gravel path to the back patio. Beneath their feet, the ground was slick with moisture, though the rain had stopped some time since she ended up in the hospital.

She looked down at her feet, picturing them walking along a similar path. No. Not gravel.

Flagstones. They were dark, barely discernible from the grass, and she'd fallen....

She lifted her hand to her head.

"Your head still hurting?"

"I fell on flagstones." She looked up at Wade and found his narrow-eyed gaze on her. "I hit my head on one."

Megan met them on the porch. The driver kept his distance. "Eric's stuck at the free clinic for the next hour or so. They had a rash of emergencies come in late. He said to get her settled in and just keep an eye on her to make sure she doesn't lose consciousness before he gets here."

Annie frowned. "You're not staying with us?"

Megan glanced at Wade before looking back at her. "We figured it would draw less attention here if we didn't do anything out of the ordinary."

"You don't want people to know you're here," Wade murmured.

She couldn't really argue that fact, she supposed. "So I'll be here alone with you? I barely know you."

"I don't reckon you know me at all," he admitted. "I've asked my cousin Cissy to come stay here, too. You'll like her. She can help you get set up with some more clothes and other woman stuff you might need."

She couldn't stop a smile at his clumsy reassurances. "Does she work for Cooper Security, too?"

"Just until she goes back to college in January," Megan answered for him.

Wade opened the door and led them into the bungalow. A slim, dark-haired woman emerged from the back of the house, followed closely by a tall, dark-haired man with sharp blue eyes. Recognition tickled the back of Annie's mind. She'd seen this woman before.

Where had she seen her before?

The brunette smiled at Annie. "You look like hell. Let's get you tucked back in bed before you fall over."

"This polite and gracious creature is my sister Isabel," Wade murmured. "Who has never been big on niceties, apparently."

"Isabel Cooper," Annie murmured, finally placing the woman. "Your partner at the FBI was killed in that bombing in Reston, Virginia."

"The reports of my death are greatly exaggerated," the blue-eyed man said with a drawl. "Ben Scanlon. Isabel's partner. Now husband."

Annie blinked with surprise. "Oh. Guess I should read my own paper more, huh?"

"We didn't exactly publicize my triumphant return to the living," Ben said with a soft laugh.

"Are you hungry?" Isabel asked. "I brought by

some leftover soup Aunt Beth made yesterday—I could microwave you a bowl."

After her nausea in the car, Annie wasn't sure she should try eating anything, but maybe a little food in her stomach might actually settle it. She had no idea when she'd last eaten—for all she knew, it could have been days.

"Aunt Beth's soup is really good," Megan coaxed. "And you might feel better once you've eaten something."

Annie's own aunt Phyllis, an amazing cook, firmly believed there was little in life that couldn't be fixed with a warm, cheesy casserole and a glass of sweet iced tea. Maybe she was right.

"Okay. I'll try some soup," she said. She turned to Wade. "Would it be okay if I borrowed your phone? I need to make a call to my aunt Phyllis, to let her know I'm okay. She must be worried sick about us."

Wade exchanged a look with his sister. Annie's stomach tightened with the tension that rose suddenly in the cozy bungalow.

"What?" she asked. "Is there something you're not telling me about my aunt Phyllis?"

"No," Wade said quickly, laying his hand on her shoulder. "As far as we know, she's just fine."

She turned to look at him. "Then what?"

"I thought you understood," he said carefully.

"Nobody else—not the police, not even your family—can know where you are."

ANNIE HARLOWE LOOKED as if she'd spent the last three weeks in hell. Her hair was dirty and tangled, still stained with her own blood. Her face was so pale it was nearly translucent. Purple shadows, dark as bruises, circled her red-rimmed eyes. And she was literally swaying on her feet as she turned fully to face Wade.

But the fire flashing from her dark eyes was hot enough to scorch him. "You're keeping me prisoner? Is that what you're saying?"

"Of course not." He kept his voice low and soothing.

She was having none of it. "So I can leave whenever I want. Go wherever I want. Talk to whomever I want. Right?"

Wade looked at his sisters for help. Isabel stepped forward, laying her hand on Annie's shoulder. "You can do any of those things, but you have to know that doing so could put you in grave danger. We might not be able to protect you."

Annie's gaze never left Wade's face. "I know I called you for help, but maybe I was hasty. The real A.F.O.S.I. will want to talk to me. Probably the FBI as well, as you pointed out earlier. I know we reporter types have a reputation of not trusting the government, but—"

"Barton Reid was once part of the government," Ben Scanlon said quietly. "He sent people to kidnap a two-year-old child from his mother to blackmail her into handing over evidence against him. He hired a whole band of mercenaries to murder a woman who'd already been tortured for her country, just to protect his own interests."

"We don't know who to trust. We're pretty sure there's at least one more person high in the government who was working with Barton Reid," Megan added. "Maybe more than one."

Annie's eyes narrowed. "The architect," she murmured.

Wade looked at Megan and Isabel. "The architect?"

Annie's eyes widened. "I don't know why I said that."

"Maybe you remembered something."

"I don't remember," she said vaguely. "I'm just so tired."

"When will Cissy get here?" Wade asked Isabel.

"She's packing a bag and should be here in the next few minutes," Isabel answered. "Annie? Would you like to take a nice long bath while we heat up the soup for you?"

The look of gratitude Annie sent Isabel's way made Wade's chest ache. God only knew what the poor woman had been through for the past three weeks. Or what fresh hell might be coming her way in the next few weeks while the search for her missing parents continued.

He waited until Isabel walked Annie back to the bathroom before he turned to Megan and Ben. "Do either of you know the results of the rape examination in the E.R.?"

Megan shook her head. "Aaron might know. He said she was conscious in the E.R. long enough to give her consent for the authorities to procure any evidence gathered during the examination."

"Good." He had a feeling that, whatever the outcome, Annie would rather know than not. He could give her at least one answer to the many questions that must be nagging her troubled mind.

"I wonder what she meant by 'the architect,'" Ben murmured.

Wade gazed toward the closed door of the bathroom. "I'm not sure she remembers. Not yet, anyway."

"The FBI is going to want to talk to her," Ben warned. A former FBI agent himself, Ben knew how the Bureau operated.

"I thought I'd call Will. The Huntsville Resident Agency would have jurisdiction in this area, and since that's where she was found—"

"Good idea," Megan agreed. "Maybe Will can arrange for a secret meeting so that nobody else in the Bureau has to know where she is."

Ben shook his head. "I can't see the FBI putting up with that kind of obfuscation for long."

"May not have to be long," Wade pointed out. "If her amnesia about the abduction is short-term, we may learn what we need to know about what happened to her and her parents in a matter of days."

ANNIE STRUGGLED TO STAY awake as the hot water enveloped her in blessed warmth, driving away many of the aches and strains that had assailed her ever since she woke in the hospital. The only bath gel Wade Cooper had in his utilitarian bathroom was something crisp and herbal, but Annie liked the scent. It reminded her of early summer in the north Georgia mountains, just before the sweltering humidity of a southern summer struck, turning even the mountains into a steam bath.

Whatever had happened to her had happened in those mountains, she thought. Someone had taken her and her parents into captivity. Bound them, she thought, lifting her hands from the water to study the ligature marks on her wrists. They still stung a little from the hot, soapy water. The marks didn't look old. They looked fresh. Still raw.

She hadn't been free from captivity for long.

Carefully, she examined the rest of her body, looking for more evidence of what had happened to her. There were bruises everywhere—her arms, her legs, her ribs. There were painful places on her back, making her wonder if she'd been beaten at some point during her captivity.

Her inner thighs appeared to be free of marks, giving her some hope that whatever else her captors had done to her, they hadn't violated her sexually. She wondered if anyone had thought to ask the doctor about her rape kit before they hurried her out of the hospital.

She wondered if she wanted to know the answer.

Releasing the trip lever to drain the tub, she pushed carefully to her feet. Tugging the shower curtain inside, she turned on the shower to rinse off, her legs trembling beneath her until she feared she'd fall. The strong spray set her scratches and abrasions to stinging again, but she found a certain raw pleasure in the sensations.

They meant she was alive. Still standing, however wobbly her legs might be at the moment.

She dried off quickly and dressed, afraid her legs would give out while she was still naked and vulnerable. Warmly ensconced in the fluffy sweats, her wet hair twisted in a towel turban-style, she sank onto the closed toilet seat and took several deep breaths to clear her foggy brain.

Had she been stupid, coming here with Wade Cooper and his family? Now that her brain had cleared a bit, she'd remembered a few things about Cooper Security—it was a fairly new company, but they were making waves in the security community. She'd even been thinking about writing a profile of them for her paper back in D.C., but for the life of her, she couldn't seem to remember why, or what angle she'd planned to pursue.

A soft knock on the door set her nerves jangling. "Annie?" The voice belonged to one of the two Cooper sisters. Not the redhead—she had a strong drawl. The other one, the FBI agent—Isabel. She had an accent, too, but not as strong. Tempered, Annie supposed, by those years working for the FBI. She'd been part of the D.C. Field Office, hadn't she? Or Baltimore, maybe. Annie couldn't remember which.

"You can come in," she called weakly.

The door eased open and Isabel stuck her head inside. "Are you okay?"

Annie nodded, bracing herself for another dizzy spell. It didn't materialize, and she released her breath. "I think so. Just a little shaky."

"You want me to help you to the bedroom?"

"No, I can do it." She pushed to her feet, pleased to find her head was starting to clear a bit. Her legs only trembled a little as she followed Isabel out of the bathroom and down the hall to a small, spare bedroom. A fluffy gray cat lay at the foot of the bed, opening his eyes as they entered. His head came up and he sniffed the air.

"Ernie, shoo," Isabel moved toward the bed. The cat just yawned.

"It's okay. I'm not allergic or anything." Annie looked at the cat. He stood slowly, arched his back for a luxurious stretch, then padded silently to the edge of the bed. He had extra toes, she saw, thumb-like appendages on his front paws and dew claws on his back. He rubbed his head against Annie's outstretched hand.

"Just be warned—Ernie will mooch your dinner."

"Ernie," she murmured. "After Ernest Hemingway?"

"Exactly," Isabel said with a smile.

Polydactyl cats were often called Hemingway cats, because the author had collected cats with extra toes. Annie's family had owned a polydactyl Maine Coon mix when she was a child. "He's sweet."

"Just be careful—he's not just a mooch but a thief," Isabel warned. "Wade says he steals things from the neighbors all the time."

Annie looked around the room, taking in the masculine decor. "Is this your brother's bedroom? I don't want to impose—"

"He was a Marine. He knows how to bunk down anywhere." Isabel pulled back the covers, making the cat jump off the bed. He disappeared out of the room in a silver flash. "He's got a foldout bed in his study for Cissy, and Wade sleeps on the sofa half the time anyway." Isabel closed her mouth suddenly, as if she'd said something she hadn't intended. "If you'd rather not sleep in those sweats, I think Megan packed a nightgown."

She still felt a little chilled and achy, and the sweats felt like an extra layer of armor against the unknown, unseen threats lurking just beyond her sight. "I'm fine with the sweats."

She slid beneath the sheets, unsurprised to find the mattress firm. *Marine,* she thought with a hidden smile. She'd lived in a military family for most of her life, her relationship with her father close and understanding. She knew soldiers, sailors, airmen and, perhaps especially, U.S. Marines found a certain pleasure in doing things the hard way, and sometimes that attitude trickled all the way down to their creature comforts.

It wasn't uncomfortable, however. She found a certain pleasure in doing things the hard way herself.

"I'll be back in a minute with the soup," Isabel said.

Annie wasn't aware of dozing off until voices outside the door jerked her awake. She heard Wade's low drawl and a second male voice, equally low but with a smoother tone that suggested a coastal southern accent rather than the hard-edged mountain twang the Coopers spoke with. She could make out little of what they were saying, except for the word *hospital.*

A moment later, she heard a light knock on the door. She pushed herself into a sitting position and said, "Come in."

Wade entered, followed by a slim, handsome man with short, dark hair and cautious blue eyes. He was carrying a large black bag—the doctor, Annie thought. He managed a smile as he walked slowly to her bedside but it faded quickly. "I'm Dr. Brannon. I work with Cooper Security. How're you feeling?"

"I'm all right," she answered as he lifted her wrist, taking obvious care not to press too firmly on her abrasions as he checked her pulse.

"Pulse is a little fast," the doctor murmured.

"Must be your good looks and charm," she said lightly, glancing at Wade. He rolled his eyes, making her smile.

"I think we've got a smart aleck on our hands," Dr. Brannon told Wade with a smile that didn't get anywhere near his watchful eyes. He lightly pinched the skin on the back of her hand, then flashed a small light in her mouth. "Mouth feels sticky and dry?"

She nodded.

"I think you're still dehydrated," he said. "I brought an IV bag—we can set you up with intravenous fluids overnight. That should get you back where you need to be."

As he pulled the IV equipment from his bag,

Wade limped over to the bed and sat on the edge. "Once he gets you hooked up, I'll get your soup. You want some crackers with it?"

Before she could answer, Dr. Brannon stepped up next to her, holding a small needle and cannula. Light glinted off the needle, and suddenly Annie was in a dark, dank place. It smelled of sweat and fear, rolling off her own aching body in waves.

"Ready, Annie?" The voice was cold. Cruel. Taking entirely too much pleasure in her distress.

The phantom burn of the pain she knew was coming was real enough to make her hyperventilate. "No!" She jerked free of her tormenter's hold, shoving him away from her. She stumbled forward, her feet tangling in her bonds. She slammed to the ground, landing hard on her shoulder.

"Annie!"

Not the same voice, she thought, trying to breathe. This voice was kind. Concerned. She twisted her body to look up and saw the warm brown eyes of Wade Cooper staring down at her, wide and scared.

The darkness melted away. She was back in the spare, clean, bright bedroom. But she was on the floor, her legs twisted up in the blanket that had covered her moments before.

Wade knelt at her side, pain evident in his furrowed brow. Sitting beside him, blotting blood from his lower lip, Dr. Brannon looked at her through narrowed eyes.

"What happened?" she asked.

"I think you just had a flashback," Wade answered.

## Chapter Five

"I don't know if you can call it post-traumatic stress disorder," Eric Brannon told Wade, Ben and Megan.

"Because the trauma is still fresh?" Wade asked.

They were in Wade's den, speaking in low tones so that Annie wouldn't hear their discussion. Isabel had stayed in the bedroom with Annie, talking to her while the injured woman ate some of the soup Isabel had reheated.

"PTSD usually manifests well after the trauma is over. I think with Ms. Harlowe, what we're seeing is ongoing trauma, just manifesting itself in odd spurts because the amnesia has obscured large chunks of what happened to her." Eric shook his head. "It's not just the marks on her wrists, either."

Wade's gut tightened. "Was she raped?"

"Unless the rape was fairly recent, you might not be able to find anything in an exam." Eric's frown deepened. "I'm talking about some marks I saw on her arms. They looked like needle marks with some skin irritation."

"They shot her up with something?" Isabel entered the den, anger coloring her voice. A few months earlier, Isabel had been kidnapped by drug runners who'd shot her up with ketamine to subdue her.

Eric lowered his voice. "I did some research on pain a while back. One investigated means of relieving pain is injections of capsaicin under the skin to overwhelm nerve pathways, relieving pain. But the initial shots—"

"Capsaicin is what makes hot peppers hot, right?" Megan looked horrified. "Someone pumped a bunch of that stuff under her skin?"

"More than once," Eric affirmed. "I saw several places on her arms. There may be places like that in other areas of her body, too."

Wade felt sick. "Why would they do that?"

"It's a crude form of torture," Eric answered. "Used short term, it doesn't leave permanent damage, but the pain is pretty damned excruciating while it's going on. Severe burning pain and, since it's subcutaneous, there's no way to wash it off and make it stop. It's sort of like shoving a bunch of jalapeño peppers under your skin and letting them do their thing."

Wade growled a profanity.

"Whoever took her must have thought she knew something about her father's secrets," Isabel's husband, Ben, said.

"Could she know anything?" Megan asked. "Do you think General Harlowe would have told his daughter anything that dangerous?"

"I don't know," Wade answered. "Maybe we should ask Annie."

"Ask me what?"

All of them turned at the sound of Annie's voice. She stood in the doorway to the den, leaning against the frame. She still looked pale, but the sallow look of illness was starting to fade away.

"You should be in bed," Wade said firmly, crossing to where she stood.

"If you're going to talk about me, do it to my face."

"Wade is right," Eric said in his best doctor voice. "You should be in bed. So let's get you back there, and then we can catch you up on what you missed while you were eating."

"I need to get home," Megan said. "Evan's going to be late getting home from the law library, and Patton's probably tearing down the cabinets trying to find something to eat." She smiled at Annie. "My dog. He's mostly a good boy, but his manners go to hell when he's hungry." She gave Isabel a hug and waggled her fingers at Wade. "Call me if you need me."

"We should probably clear out, too," Ben said, catching Isabel's hand in his. "I just heard from

Cissy while y'all were in the bedroom. She's on her way, so we should leave and give her room to park."

Isabel smiled at Annie. "If you need anything, you let me know, okay? Wade can give you my number."

Annie managed a wan smile. "Thank you. You've all been so kind."

Wade walked his sisters and Ben out onto the porch. "Can one of you email me everything we have on Annie Harlowe?" he asked quietly.

Isabel's eyes narrowed. "Those files should be on the web archive by now. I think Shannon uploaded the latest information we have this morning."

"Good." The more he knew about his new ward, the better. He hadn't been directly involved in the search for Annie in Georgia, thanks to his bad knee, so he didn't know a lot about the missing people. It was time to give himself a crash course in all things Annie Harlowe.

Inside, he found Eric Brannon sitting next to Annie on the sofa, pointing out the red spots on her arm. "There are probably other places on your body where the skin will be red like that, so try not to freak out about them if you find them. They'll go away in a few days and your pain receptors will get back to normal."

Annie met Wade's gaze. She looked more angry than upset. "Those bastards tortured me."

He eased into the seat across from her. "I know. I'm sorry."

"What did they think they were going to accomplish? I'm not a spy. I don't have the secrets of the universe hidden in my brain."

Wade remembered something she'd said when he's first found her. She'd been delirious and not even half-conscious, but she'd murmured, "I don't know where it is."

"The torture might not have been for your benefit," Eric said grimly.

"They may have tortured me to get my father to tell them something?"

"It makes sense." Wade leaned forward, resting his forearms on his knees. "I think that could be the reason they took you and your mother captive as well as your father."

"But he's retired now. He isn't even in the Air Force anymore, as of June of this year. What secrets do they really think they'll get from him? Anything highly classified was probably revised and recoded once he was out. The military isn't big on taking those kinds of chances with secrets."

"Maybe there was some other sort of secret your father was hiding," Wade suggested carefully. It was possible Annie Harlowe knew nothing about the coded journal his sister Shannon had discover a few weeks ago, a journal that had belonged to one of General Harlowe's closest friends.

General Edward Ross had been, like General Harlowe, one of three generals in charge of the peacekeeping mission in the Central Asian nation of Kaziristan. From what Cooper Security had pieced together over the past few months, the three generals had begun to suspect that high-ranking individuals in the U.S. government were cutting their own deals with al Adar rebels in Kaziristan in hopes of influencing the governmental composition of the oil-rich nation.

Unfortunately, General Ross himself was dead, the victim of what was looking more and more like foul play designed to appear as an ordinary car crash. And without Ross to decode the journal, Cooper Security was no closer to finding out what, exactly, the three generals knew.

They had hoped the other two generals, Harlowe and Marsh, might be able to answer some of their questions, but Harlowe and his family had gone missing around the same time Shannon had found the journal. And Baxter Marsh was being anything but cooperative with Cooper Security at the moment.

"If he had any secrets," she said, " I don't know what they could be."

"Well," Eric said, standing up, "that's a subject you need to table, at least for tonight. I'm not going to risk getting your blood pressure up again by trying to put you on IV fluids, but that means you need to drink plenty of fluids, starting now." He turned to Wade. "You need to check on her every couple of hours."

"You mean wake me up every few hours to make sure I'm not in a coma," Annie grumbled.

The doctor shot her an apologetic look. "Exactly."

"I'll take care of her," Wade said firmly. He felt Annie's gaze on him and slanted a look her way. She was studying him through narrowed eyes as if trying to figure out his angle.

He almost laughed aloud. He had no angle. He was probably the simplest, most straightforward of all the Coopers. No inscrutable motives like Jesse or hidden depths like Isabel. He didn't possess a genius brain like Shannon or the chameleon-like charm of his brother Rick. Of all his siblings, he was the most like his sister Megan, and even down-home country girl Megan had more layers than he did.

He waited until Eric had left to speak. "I don't have a lot to offer in the way of juice. There's apple juice in the fridge, and water of course."

"Water's fine."

He limped into the kitchen and dug in the cabinet until he found a thirty-two-ounce water bottle with a drinking nozzle. "Iced or tap?"

"Iced." Her voice was impossibly close, making him jerk with surprise. He turned to find her only a couple of feet away, one hand holding on to the kitchen bar, as if she needed its support to stay upright. "I can get it."

He shook his head. "You need to be in bed resting. Why don't you go ahead and get settled and I'll bring you the water."

Her eyes narrowed again. "What's in this for you?"

"You need help. That's what Cooper Security does."

"For a price."

He inclined his head toward her, conceding her point. "In this case, we're hoping for a little information."

"From me?"

"Maybe. Hopefully from your father."

His answer seemed to confuse her. "What kind of information?"

He hadn't yet been given the go-ahead to tell Annie Harlowe about the coded journal. Knowledge of its whereabouts had nearly gotten his sister killed only a couple of weeks ago. The mercenaries looking for the journal—and, Wade assumed, the high-powered men who'd hired them to find it—almost certainly knew that Cooper Security now had the journal. It was one reason Jesse had raised the security level at the offices.

Annie swayed on her feet, steadying herself on the side of the refrigerator. Wade set down the bottle of iced water and caught her before she slid to the floor.

She rested her forehead against his shoulder a moment, then lifted her face to look at him. Tears trickled from her eyelids. She dashed them away. "Damn it."

"Don't try to recover all at once," Wade murmured, remembering his own frustration with his slow rate of recovery after his injury. "One step at a time. And the first step needs to be rest." He tightened his grip on her, trying to ignore the soft curves that even three weeks of captivity hadn't starved away from her. She was built the way he liked a woman, fit but curvy, with full breasts, generous hips and a little meat on her bones.

"I don't have time to wait." Pushing out of his arms, she grabbed the edge of the counter to maintain her balance and gazed up at him. Desperation lined her face. "I have to find my family."

"And we'll help you with that. But tonight, you need to rest. I'll call Eric and see if there's something he can give you to help you sleep."

She shook her head. "No. I don't want anything. Head injury, remember?"

"Oh. Right." He picked up the water bottle and screwed on the cap. "Well, let's get you settled." He glanced at his watch—well after midnight now. "I'll set my alarm to get me up around two-thirty to check on you."

She grimaced. "Is that really necessary?"

"Doctor's orders."

She slanted a look at him. "Do you always do what you're told?"

"Rarely," he admitted with a grin. "But I do when it makes sense."

She gave him another one of her narrow-eyed looks. He was getting used to it. Clearly she was one of those people who figured everyone had a hidden agenda. He supposed she had a right—she had been living and working in the nation's capital for five years, according to her dossier. She was a reporter for one of the papers there, on the political beat. That was surely enough to make anyone a fire-breathing cynic.

A knock on the door set his nerves on edge. It made Annie visibly flinch. She reached out a shaking hand toward him before dropping it back to her side.

"Probably my cousin," he reassured her. He walked to the door and checked through the peephole. His young cousin stood outside, looking solemn and intense.

He opened the door. "Hey, Scooter."

She rolled her eyes at the nickname. "Where is she?"

"I'm here." Annie spoke quietly behind him. Turning, he found her standing straight and steady, though the grinding of her jaw muscles and the clenching of her fists showed what an effort it was taking for her to remain upright. "You must be Cissy."

Cissy smiled, but it was halfhearted. She'd had a personal trauma a few months earlier, losing her first serious boyfriend and what was left of her innocence in one cruel blow. Gone was the eager, excited girl who'd been looking forward to applying to the FBI as soon as she graduated college. This older, wiser Cissy Cooper was quieter. Gloomier. But she was also stronger and more mature. Finding out the guy you loved was a murderer could do that to a person, Wade supposed.

"It's really late. We should all be in bed," Cissy said firmly. She set her overnight bag on the floor by the sofa. "Who's sleeping where?"

"You've got the foldout in the study. Annie has the bed, and I'll sleep here on the sofa."

"Okay." Cissy looked at Annie. "You catch me up on your condition and what we have to do to get you back to your old self. Wade, can you take my bag to the study?" Cissy led Annie out of the living room.

With a bemused smile, Wade picked up the suitcase and carried it to the study. As he set about unfolding the pullout sofa for his cousin, he could hear soft conversation going on in the bedroom, too low for him to make out any words.

Taking a chance his cousin was still awake after

the evening's excitement, he punched in Aaron's cell phone number.

Aaron answered on the first ring. "You're still up?"

"About to bunk down," Wade answered. "I just wanted to check on something—did the rape exam done on Annie Harlowe turn up anything?"

"I'm not supposed to share that with anybody outside law enforcement."

"Well, could you tell her? I know it's eating at her." He walked to the bedroom and found the door ajar. Cissy was sitting on the edge of the bed, looking at the red blotches Annie was showing her.

They both looked up as Wade entered. Cissy's eyes burned with bleak fury. "Can you believe what they did to her?"

Sadly, after all they'd learned about the S.S.U. over the past couple of years, he could believe their depravity with unsettling ease. "Annie, I've got my cousin Aaron on the phone. He has the results of the rape exam."

Her expression froze, but he saw fear in her eyes. Taking a deep breath, she held out her hand for the phone. Wade handed it over, and she put the phone to her ear. "This is Annie Harlowe."

She listened for a moment, her expression unchanged. Then she swallowed hard, said, "Thank you," to Aaron and handed the phone back to Wade.

She took another deep breath and murmured, "Negative."

Wade felt a little of the tension in his back unwind. He put the phone in his pocket. "That's good, isn't it?"

Annie pulled the covers up over her, tucking her knees up to her chest. "It means I wasn't raped in the last little while. I'm not sure it can be definitive about the last three weeks. And I can't remember any of it."

"My aunt Hannah had a concussion and lost some of her memory, but she got it all back eventually," Cissy said. "It can happen for you, too."

"I wish it would happen soon. I can't stand not knowing, especially with my parents in danger." Her expression fell. "If they're even still alive."

"I think they must be," Wade said carefully. He didn't want to give her false hope just for the hell of it—believing a lie never did a person any good in the end. But everything he knew about the three generals suggested that the S.S.U. would be under orders to keep General Harlowe alive.

The best cryptographers Cooper Security had on staff had agreed with Wade's sister Shannon's assessment: General Ross's coded journal would probably require input from the other two generals to decode. With General Ross dead, it would be that much more vital for the S.S.U. to keep General Harlowe and General Marsh alive. They'd made a grave error in killing General Ross. It wasn't a mistake they'd make twice if they could avoid it.

They'd kept Annie alive for three weeks, apparently using her as leverage against her father. Her escape made it all the more likely that they'd keep Mrs. Harlowe alive as well. She was the only piece of leverage they had left, with Annie out of the picture.

"I think we should all get some sleep." Cissy tugged Wade's arm.

Wade shot a smile at Annie. "See you in a couple of hours."

To his pleasure, she made a face at him, a hint of a smile curving her pale lips. *That's more like it*, he thought.

He followed Cissy out and closed the door behind him.

"She looks like hell," Cissy said when they reached the study. "No wonder she fears what she can't remember. What we know is bad enough."

"I appreciate your coming tonight. Above and beyond the call of duty."

Cissy's expression darkened. "I hate those S.S.U. sons of bitches."

He squeezed her shoulder. "I reckon you would."

She leaned against his arm and he pulled her into a bear hug. After a moment, she wriggled free and shot him a saucy grin, the first real smile he'd seen from her in days. "Why don't we take turns with the wake-up call? You can take the first one, and I'll set my alarm clock for four hours from now?"

"You don't have to do that—"

"I don't mind." Cissy picked up her overnight bag. "Go get some sleep yourself. Two hours will come fast."

Wade headed for the living room, nearly tripping over Ernie. "Don't like sleeping with a pretty woman?" he asked the cat.

Ernie jumped up on the sofa, his green eyes gleaming.

Wade set his alarm clock for two hours later, turned off the light and stretched out on the sofa, groaning as his knee seized up briefly as he stretched it out. Ernie curled up on Wade's side, purring loudly. The cat had become bold over the past few weeks, making himself right at home inside the house. Wade should probably quit pretending he didn't really have a cat.

He stared up at the ceiling, where faint light from outside washed over it. Used to being alone, he keenly felt the presence of the two other women now sleeping under his roof. Both of them gave him ample reasons to worry, Cissy with her broken heart and broken spirit, and Annie Harlowe with her battered body, foggy mind and danger hanging over her like a black cloud. They both needed a champion.

A hero.

But Wade was afraid he wasn't hero material anymore.

# Chapter Six

"The code. Where is it?"

Annie squinted against the bright lamp. Her head hurt, her skin felt as if it were on fire, and the light stabbed her aching eyes like brilliant knives. "I don't know what you're talking about." Her throat felt raw and dry, her voice little more than a croak.

"Don't pretend your daddy didn't tell you." The voice belonged to a man, the broad Louisiana drawl reminding her of her cousins from Houma. But she'd never heard this man's voice before. She'd have remembered it.

"Where's my father?" she asked, fear strangling her.

"He sends his love," her captor replied with a sneering smile in his voice. His face was hidden behind the utility light shining in her face, his features impossible to make out. He was only a voice, a hateful, sneering growl that chilled her to the bone.

"Where's my mother?"

"She's safe. For now but your daddy won't tell

us anything," the man continued. "So you have to do it for him. Save him, 'cause the old bastard's not going to save himself."

That wasn't true, either, Annie thought through the fog inhabiting her brain. He had to have told them something, or they wouldn't know about the code at all. She couldn't believe anything her captor said, she realized. Not a word that came out of this man's mouth could be trusted as the truth.

*Protect the code.* That's what her father had said. She could hear his growling drawl, as if he were speaking directly into her ear. "Whatever happens, whoever demands answers, you must protect the code."

"Annie?" Another voice spoke behind the light. A warm, drawling voice that made her chest ache with relief. "Annie, time to wake up again."

She opened her eyes and the bright light was gone, replaced by the soft glow of morning light seeping in through the bedroom windows. Next to her, Wade Cooper's body was a warm, solid reality so welcome after her nightmare that she wanted to fling herself into his arms and bury her face in his broad chest.

She resisted the urge, pushing her hair out of her face. "I'm awake."

Wade gently checked her pulse. "Heart rate's a little high."

"I was having a nightmare," she admitted,

though she couldn't remember more than a snippet of it now. Just a voice, her father's rumbling words, spoken in a near whisper.

*Protect the code.*

"Do you remember anything about it?"

She almost told him. But something inside, a clawing terror that nearly stole her breath, silenced her. "Not really."

"Feel like moving around a little?" He held his hand out to her.

She took it, shivering as his big, warm hand closed over hers, and let him help her into a sitting position on the edge of the bed. The last couple of times she'd awakened, first with Wade, then with Cissy, she'd felt dizzy and more than a little queasy. But at the moment, she almost felt normal. And starving.

"I think I might be hungry." She shot Wade a lopsided grin.

He smiled. "Good thing Cissy's in there fixing breakfast, then."

She could smell it now, the unmistakable aroma of bacon frying. "Y'all trying to fatten me up?" she asked, falling effortlessly into the coastal Carolina drawl of her childhood.

His smile quirked. "Where'd that accent come from?"

"Charleston, South Carolina," she answered with

a self-conscious smile. "Our home base. My parents are both from there."

"It's nice." Wade stood, grimacing as he put weight on his bad knee. "Check the closet. Apparently Isabel scavenged spare outfits from all the Cooper girls close to your size. No telling what you'll find."

What she found were several sets of jeans, shirts and a couple of light sweaters. The clothes were all a little loose on her but in no danger of falling off, and given how eagerly her stomach was growling at the smell of frying bacon, she had a feeling her clothes would need to be as loose as possible for all the food she intended to wolf down as soon as she reached the kitchen.

She didn't quite make it all the way through the bacon and cheese omelet Cissy plated for her before her stomach protested, but she did manage to down a whole glass of apple juice. By the time Dr. Brannon dropped by around nine to check on her, she felt almost like her old self.

"Greatly improved," he pronounced with a look of satisfaction. "You're making me look like a medical superhero, Ms. Harlowe."

"I feel better," she conceded. "Think I can go outside for a while?"

Wade shook his head. "You know you can't go out."

"Not even for a walk?" She looked longingly at

the sun shining outside the living room window. "I don't know where I was kept, but I doubt I got much fresh air or sunshine. I'm sure I'll feel loads better if I can move around and get some sun. I'm probably vitamin D deficient by now." She looked away from Wade and addressed the doctor. "Tell him I need sunshine."

"I know you want to keep her under wraps," Dr. Brannon said over his shoulder to Wade. "But she's right. There's only one other house in the immediate area, right? And it's empty at the moment."

Wade looked inclined to nix the idea, which grated on her nerves. "Am I your prisoner?" she asked, reprising a question she'd asked the night before.

His expression shifted. "No. Of course not."

"You can come with me. Watch my back."

Wade glanced at Cissy. She shrugged.

"Okay. But when I say it's time to come back inside, no arguing."

"Deal." She was surprised by how excited she was at the prospect of a stroll around the lake house. Just how far had her life devolved over the past three weeks that she'd find the idea of a simple stroll so stimulating?

By the time she and Wade had wandered a hundred yards from his house, she had her answer. It had devolved a lot. The muscles in her legs screamed and burned, and she was nearly out of breath.

"My first physical therapy session after the surgeons put my leg back together was hell." Wade stopped to lean against a pine tree trunk.

She leaned against one a few feet away, grateful for the chance to rest and catch her breath. "How'd you hurt your leg?"

"Al Adar rebels shot me in the kneecap," he answered flatly.

She winced. "Damn."

"The knee was a loss, but the surgeons worked hard to save the leg."

"How long ago?" The headline-grabbing siege in Kaziristan had happened several years ago, but she knew the fighting had gone on a lot longer than that. There were still some NATO troops left in Kaziristan, including American soldiers, trying to keep the stabilizing nation from devolving into chaos again.

"Two years," he answered. "The doctors promise I'll continue getting better." He sounded as if he didn't believe it.

"Does it hurt?"

"Not all the time. Just when I overuse it. Or I try to kneel or crouch or, you know, treat it like a working knee." The bitterness in his voice rang loud and clear. He shot her a sheepish look. "Not that I feel sorry for myself or anything."

"We're a pair," she said with a smile. "You're all bitter and gimpy and I'm muddle-headed and weak as a kitten."

He laughed aloud, as if surprised by her blunt candor. "Bitter and gimpy, huh?" He pushed away from the tree trunk and patted the pistol he had tucked into a waistband holster attached to his jeans. "Well, that's where the Glock comes in handy. The great equalizer."

She eyed the gun, realizing for the first time that she'd allowed herself to go out in the woods alone with an armed stranger. Just how desperate had she become to find someone to trust?

Even now, with the possibility of treachery placed firmly in her head, she didn't feel afraid of Wade Cooper. Every instinct she had told her he was one of the good guys.

But could she really trust her instincts, with so much of her memory missing?

She fell into step with him, trying to stay focused and aware as they walked farther into the woods. Even if Wade Cooper was one of the good guys, she couldn't depend on him—or anyone else—to protect her.

Her parents were in trouble. And the key to finding them was locked somewhere in her brain. She was their only hope. Not Wade Cooper or his family or anyone else.

If her parents were to be found, it was up to her to find them.

With her mind occupied with the crushing weight of that thought, she didn't realize immediately that they'd moved out of thick woods into a partial clearing. Almost blending into the woods around them stood a large, wood-shingled house. It took her a minute to realize where she was.

The Marshes' lake house.

It had been a long time since she'd visited this place. Over ten years ago, at least. She'd been a bright-eyed high school graduate, less than a month away from her first year at the University of Georgia. She'd picked journalism as her major, much to her mother's pride and her father's chagrin. The older Marsh girl, Rita, had been a junior at Yale and, if Annie recalled correctly, mooning over some young Marine Corps lieutenant under her father's command. She'd tried to convince Annie that an Ivy League school would be the smarter choice and seemed downright horrified that Annie had turned down an offer from Columbia to choose the Grady School of Journalism and Mass Communications at Georgia instead.

Evie, the younger Marsh, had been seventeen and tomboyish. She'd secretly confided to Annie that she wanted to join the Marine Corps, but her father wouldn't hear of it. Annie had never heard whether or not Evie had gotten her wish. General

Marsh had changed commands at that point, and the Marsh and Harlowe families had lost touch for a while.

She was surprised she even remembered the place, but as they walked slowly around to the front of the house, she had a strong flash of memory.

Rain, pouring in sheets. The empty facade of the house staring back at her like a slumbering beast, daring her to wake it.

But she had to get inside.

*Get General Marsh. General Marsh can help.*

Her legs wobbled beneath her, and she took a stumbling step forward to keep her balance. Her toe caught on one of the flagstones half hidden in the deep grass, pitching her forward.

Wade caught her before she fell, dragging her into his tight embrace.

She twisted in his arms, looking up at him, a flood of memories rattling her brain. She'd tripped on one of the flagstones and fallen, hitting her head. Blood had dripped like water into her face, she remembered. It had hurt like hell, but she couldn't stand still.

They were looking for her.

"I hit my head on a flagstone," she said aloud, her voice oddly distant, as if she were speaking from far away.

"One of these flagstones?" Wade's arms tightened around her. "I found you not far from here—"

"I think I was here last night." She found her balance again, and Wade let her go. Cool morning air seeped into her clothes, replacing the earlier warmth of his arms. She felt strangely bereft.

"Here at this lake house?"

"Yes."

"Do you know why you were here? Did someone drop you off?"

She heard an engine rumbling in her head. "A truck."

"Someone let you out of a truck? Just dropped you off?"

She couldn't let anyone see her. She had to be sure nobody saw her. The fear of discovery was so strong, it made her insides tremble even now. "No, I don't think they dropped me off. I think I stowed away and got out on my own."

Wade's brow furrowed. "You stowed away on a truck?"

"I think so." She pressed the heels of her hands to her forehead, struggling to remember. "I think it was the only way I could get here."

"Here to the lake house?"

She looked up at the silent face of the house, at the low-slung front porch and the solid wood door. "Yes."

She'd needed to see General Marsh. General Marsh could help.

But help her do what?

"I don't remember why," she said aloud, although in the back of her mind, she heard her father's plea.

*Protect the code.*

"I'm tired," she said, tucking the thought away. She'd think about it later, when she was alone. She wasn't a good liar. If she wasn't careful, Wade Cooper would see through her deceit.

*You can trust him, can't you? He's taken care of you so far.*

But he was still a stranger.

She couldn't trust anyone. Not with her parents' lives on the line.

ANNIE HARLOWE WAS keeping secrets. Wade could see it in the way her face shuttered during her moments of silence. It was if there was a whole mysterious world inside her brain, a movie playing out behind her soft caramel eyes that she kept hidden from the rest of the world.

How much of it was natural reticence, and how much was active deception? Wade couldn't be sure, not yet. But if there was one thing he was still good at, one thing the al Adar bullet hadn't stolen from him, it was his natural instinct for ferreting out the truth.

Once, when Jesse hadn't known he was in earshot, Wade had heard his older brother refer to him as "the Cooper Security lie detector." Jesse would never have said it to his face—the eldest Cooper brother liked to keep his younger siblings humble by rationing his praise in small, timely doses.

But Wade *was* pretty good at detecting bull. And right now, Annie Harlowe was chock full of bull, at least where her memory was concerned.

She remembered something. Maybe a lot of somethings. And General Marsh's lake house figured right in the middle of it all.

He didn't think she was lying about having been at the Marsh's house the night before. Wade had found her in the woods about forty yards uphill from the lakeside cabin. The gash in her forehead could have easily come from falling and hitting her head on the edge of the flagstone, as she'd said.

But he had a feeling she knew why she'd ended up at the Marshes' lake house, and that was the part of her memory she seemed determined not to share with the rest of them. He supposed it was natural that she'd be reticent where her inner secrets were concerned. Despite the help they'd given her, she really didn't know the Coopers from any set of strangers she might run into on the street.

And he hadn't exactly been sharing any of his secrets with her, had he?

The Coopers had been sitting on General Ross's coded journal for weeks, not sharing what they knew with anyone outside the handful of Cooper Security agents who needed to know what they had in their possession. Even the bad guys could only guess that the Coopers had control of the journal.

It was a secret Jesse had entrusted to a chosen few, and Wade had told no one else about it.

But watching Annie Harlowe sitting on the sofa, deep in thoughts he wished he had the power to read, Wade was beginning to think the secret of the journal might be just the thing that would convince Annie to spill a few of her own secrets.

They were already certain that General Harlowe had known about Ross's journal. If Wade's sister Shannon and her boyfriend Gideon were right, Harlowe himself, along with Baxter Marsh, might be the only people left who knew how to decode the journal and reveal its tantalizing secrets.

The phone rang, making Annie jump. She shot a sheepish grin at Wade as he crossed to the side table to pick up the phone. No ID on the display panel on the phone. Probably the office. "Hello?"

He was right. Jesse was on the other end of the call, and he sounded tense. "We've just had an incident."

Wade listened, glancing toward Annie as his brother tersely described an unexpected visit from a man in uniform to the Cooper Security offices.

"It wasn't one of the men from the hospital," Jesse said, "but we do know he's not an S.S.U. agent. At least, not as far as we've been able to ascertain." Jesse described a short, stocky man in his mid-forties, with thinning blond hair and sharp blue eyes.

The description didn't ring any bells for Wade, but apparently his brother's wife Amanda, who'd once been a CIA operative, had recognized the man as a fellow spook.

"Says his name is Oliver Pennock, and the last she knew, he was pretty high up in the Transnational Issues Division. Said his area of expertise was Central Asia."

"Kaziristan," Wade murmured.

Annie's gaze snapped to his face, her entire body going tense, and he regretted speaking aloud.

"He came here looking for Annie Harlowe," Jesse said. "He asked all friendly-like, smiling and easygoing, but when we told him to talk to the Chickasaw County Sheriff's Department, he dropped the act. Pretty much threatened our company, our business license, and most of our staff with all sorts of dire, unspoken consequences if we didn't turn her over to him."

"What did you tell him?"

"What do you think?"

Wade grinned, imagining just how many creative places his brother, the ultimate Marine, had suggested the CIA agent stuff his threats.

"That does mean he knows we have her," Jesse warned, wiping the smile off Wade's face. "I don't think she's going to be safe there with you much longer."

Wade looked at Annie again, his stomach tightening with dread. She'd just begun to look a little bit settled around here, and he was about to have to uproot her once again. "Who's going to get her out of here?"

Annie sat up, swinging her legs over the edge of the couch. The look she sent his way was full of alarm.

"You are," Jesse answered firmly.

A ripple of panic shot through his gut. "Alone?"

"We're pretty sure we're being watched here at the office. You need to get her out of there as soon as you can. Head for the Cooper Cove Marina— I'll call Uncle Mike to let him know y'all are coming. Dad's down there this morning, helping out at the bait shop, so he can help you figure out what comes next. But you need to get away from your house now."

"Okay. I'll call back from the bait shop—"

"No. I'm not sure the office phones are safe. I'm using an untraceable phone, so I'll call you." Jesse hung up without saying goodbye.

"We have to get out of here, don't we?"

Wade turned to look at Annie, who was now on her feet. She still looked a little pale, a little tired, but there was also an undercurrent of energy flowing through her, electric even from the distance of a few feet. Wade felt drawn to that core of strength radiating from her, as if he could pull from that energy to fill his own flagging resources. He took a couple of steps toward her before he stopped himself.

"I know you need more rest—"

She shook her head, cutting him off. "Just catch me up on what's happened while I pack."

THE COOPER COVE MARINA nestled in a wide-mouthed cove about five miles from Wade Cooper's bungalow. The marina itself consisted of five large piers from which jutted several boat slips, many of them occupied. As Annie followed Wade up the gravel path to the small bait shop a few yards inland from the piers, she saw a couple of boats slide in expertly to adjacent slips. Two dark-haired men who looked almost identical tied up their boats with the speed of experts and headed down the pier toward them.

Wade gave a wave but didn't stop to greet them. The two men waved back and kept coming. Annie felt an unexpected fear of turning her back on the strangers, even though Wade seemed to recognize them.

"This is awfully exposed," she murmured to him as they reached the front door of the bait shop.

"That's why we have to act like we're not trying to hide," Wade responded with equal softness.

"But if you're worried about those guys following us, relax. They're my cousins, and they hate the S.S.U. every bit as much as you do."

Wade led her up to the front counter, where two men in their mid-sixties stood together, watching them arrive in silent scrutiny. The taller of the two men smiled a greeting, but the other man, Annie noticed, was watching Wade's limping struggle with a hint of dismay.

"Dad, Uncle Mike, this is Annie." Waving toward the taller man, Wade said, "Annie, my uncle Mike. And this," he added, looking at the shorter man," is my dad, Roy Cooper."

"Nice meeting you, Annie," Roy Cooper said with a genuine smile. He turned his gaze to his son. "Hear you need a quick getaway."

Wade's smile didn't quite make it to his eyes. "Word gets around fast on the Cooper grapevine."

"Jesse called to arrange for you to take a boat trip across the lake to Willow Point. Jake's going to drive you over there, and Gabe's riding shotgun to watch your back."

"And what happens when we get to Willow Point?"

"Mariah will pick you up and take you to Luke's stable," one of Wade's cousins answered. Either Jake or Gabe. Annie didn't know which was which, or if she'd have been able to tell them apart if she did.

Wade gave his cousin an odd look. "You don't expect us to ride horses out of here, do you?"

The other cousin laughed. "Lord, no. Like Luke would let you have any of his horses anyway. No, they're going to let you borrow the stable truck. They don't have any need to haul horses over the next few days, so it'll just be sitting there in the yard unused anyway. And it's Riley Patterson's old truck, so it's not even registered to anyone named Cooper."

Wade clapped the man's shoulder. "You, Gabe Cooper, are a genius."

"It was my idea," the other cousin protested.

"You're a genius, too, Jake." Wade turned to Annie, his dark eyes glittering with life. He was excited by the prospect of the unknown adventure spreading out like a big, wild mystery in front of them, she realized. Even though it might be—no, almost certainly would be—dangerous. Maybe he was excited *because* it was certain to be dangerous.

Even stranger, some of his excitement seemed to have infected her as well, because the idea of going on the run with Wade Cooper had her knees trembling and her heart pounding, not with fear but with anticipation.

Had she utterly lost her mind? Or was it the sheer relief of doing something active, even if it was running away from the bad guys, that had her blood flowing like fire in her veins?

For three nearly blank weeks of her life, she'd apparently been a mouse in a cage, tormented and trapped and utterly helpless. Now she was free. Running for her life, scared out of her wits, but free.

It was about damned time.

The ride across the lake took only a few minutes. They met up with a beautiful woman with dark brown hair and silvery eyes—Mariah, the wife of Wade's cousin Jake—who smiled a quiet greeting before she quickly herded them into her SUV. Another ten-minute drive down a winding country road ended at a sprawling stable yard.

A tall man with buzz-cut dark hair emerged from the barn. He waved Mariah off, and she drove away. "Luke Cooper," he introduced himself to Annie quickly. "Sure am glad to see you alive and kicking."

Annie managed a smile in return, though she was already starting to feel overwhelmed. So much for her earlier flash of bravery.

"Here are the keys." Luke handed Wade a small key ring with two keys on it. "Try not to wreck it and don't get pulled over. You're not covered on the insurance policy."

"I think that's the least of our worries," Wade said with a wry smile.

Luke looked at Annie again, but he addressed the question to his cousin. "Any clue where you're going?"

"Don't know." Wade looked at Annie. "Any idea how we're supposed to stay in touch?"

"Oh, yeah. Nearly forgot." Luke dug in his pocket and pulled out a small, nondescript cell phone. "Prepaid, untraceable. Use it sparingly."

Wade took the phone. "Thanks. For everything."

They walked to the other side of the barn, where a dusty forest-green Ram 1500 pickup truck sat next to a large bale of hay. "So," Wade said as he unlocked the passenger door. "Where you reckon we should go?"

Annie had been thinking about that question ever since they hopped aboard his cousin's bass boat back at the marina. "I think there's really only one place that makes sense."

He paused in the middle of shoving the duffel bags containing their supplies into the bench seat of the truck. "Yeah? Where's that?"

"I think we need to go back to north Georgia."

Where the whole horrible mess had begun.

## Chapter Seven

"This is a really bad idea." Wade eyed the main drag of Pea Hollow, Georgia, population 350, and felt like a ten-point buck in a wide-open field. He could practically feel the eyes on them as they drove along Main Street, heading for the mountain pass.

"No risk, no reward," Annie said in a gritty drawl.

"We could have come from the opposite direction. Skipped town."

"We always drive through town when we come here. If I'm going to remember anything that happened after I arrived at the Chattanooga Airport, I think I need to re-create my steps back here." Annie dipped Wade's baseball cap lower on her forehead. "We usually stop at The Sweeterie because Mom swears their pecan pralines are the best around." Her voice hitched slightly, drawing his gaze to her face again. She peered forward through the windshield, her lips trembling briefly. "I like the pistachio clusters better."

"Well, I'd offer to stop and buy you a bag, but—"

She managed a grim smile. "Yeah, low profile. I know."

"Then again, if you usually stop somewhere, maybe that's what we should do," Wade said, torn between wanting answers and wanting to keep Annie safe. "You don't have to get out, but maybe I could take a look around. I could put my cell phone camera on video record. You could watch the video and see if it triggers any memories."

She gave him a quick, appreciative look. "Good idea. Let's do it."

He felt appallingly pleased with himself for winning her approval. "Okay, so, is the sweet shop the first place you stop?"

She slanted a look at him. "Two women. A store full of chocolate. What do you think?"

He grinned. "Okay, point me toward the chocolate."

She guided him to a small storefront across from the post office. *The Sweeterie* was painted in whimsical lettering across the glass window. "It's small, so you should be able to video the whole shop in about a minute. You know, be obvious about it. Make up a story or something about why you're filming."

He frowned. He might be good at seeing through

a lie, but he wasn't very good at creating one. "Like what?"

"Like, you came up here to go fishing with friends, and your girlfriend had to work and couldn't make it," she suggested. "So you promised you'd film your trip to the chocolate shop so it would be just like she was there." She darted another look at Wade. "And you bought a bag of pistachio clusters to take home to her."

He laughed aloud. "To maintain the cover."

"Of course."

If a bag of pistachio clusters would maintain that smile on her face, even a little while, they'd be worth every penny he paid for them.

He walked a full circuit of the chocolate shop, filming the counter, the display cases, even some of the customers. As expected, the curiosity of the ponytailed clerk behind the counter forced him to explain the cover story. The clerk thought he was adorably devoted to his girlfriend and even threw in an extra half pound of pistachio clusters.

"Apparently being a sap gets you extra chocolate," he told Annie as she exclaimed over the amount of candy he'd purchased.

"It's not sappy. It's sweet and considerate. You must have sold it really well, Cooper."

Again he felt a flood of pleasure at her smiling approbation. "Well, I'm telling you now, I'm not holding your purse at the mall."

She laughed, the first lighthearted sound he'd heard from her since she'd awakened at the hospital in Chickasaw County. "Duly noted."

He handed her his phone as he pulled out into the late afternoon traffic on Main Street. "I pretty much covered the whole place. It's the untitled one at the end."

She found the video archive and started playing, grinning a little as she listened to his stuttering explanation of his reason for filming the shop. But her grin faded suddenly, and her body went rigid, straining against the seat belt. The phone tumbled to the floorboard at her feet as her hands came up, clawing at the restraint. She let out a low, keening moan.

They were past the edge of town now, moving into the wooded access road up the mountain to the Pea Hollow cabins. He had to wait until he could find a shoulder wide enough to accommodate the truck before he could pull over and check on her.

"Annie?" He put his hand on her shoulder.

She jerked at his touch, letting out a howl of terror.

SHE COULDN'T MOVE, tethered in place by steel cables strapped to hooks in the wall. She'd escaped her restraints before, sawing through the plastic cuffs they'd used the first time, then twisting free of the ropes they'd used as replacements for the flex cuffs.

They weren't going to let her escape again.

"Let me go!" she howled at the darkness, not because she felt anyone there, as she often did, but because the sound of her voice made her feel marginally less impotent.

"Annie, stop."

That wasn't a voice she knew. It was a kind voice. A scared voice.

She realized her hands were free. She tugged at the bands holding her in place, puzzled to find not corded steel but woven nylon. They gave as she pulled, giving her room to pitch herself forward. But something still held her trapped at the waist.

*This isn't right. This isn't what happened.*

A tiny voice of sanity murmured in the back of her head, but her panic drowned it out. She pulled desperately at the nylon strap holding her captive, running her hand over the fabric.

She felt hands on her, trying to hold her in place. She slapped at the hands, blind but terrified.

And in the blackness inside her head, she heard her father's voice. "If you get out of here, find Marsh."

She pushed against the hands again, redoubling her effort to find a way free of the strap holding her hips pinned to the wall. Her fingers brushed over steel—a buckle. She pushed down on a moving part and the buckle fell away, freeing her from her captivity.

She turned away from the grasping hands and crashed into something hard, headfirst. She cried out as pain streaked through her head, filling the darkness in her mind with sparkling lights.

"Annie, stop!" Hands caught her again, pulling her back against a warm, hard body.

She could see again, light so bright it made her eyes burn. The ache in her head subsided to a dull throb, and she realized she wasn't in a darkened room at all.

She was in a truck. The wall closing her in was the passenger door.

And the body wrapped around hers, keeping her firmly in place, belonged to Wade Cooper.

She twisted in his arms, looking into his fathomless eyes to reassure herself that she was right. It was him. He stared back at her, breathing hard. "Annie? Are you hearing me?"

"I'm back," she said, her throat feeling sore and raspy.

His big hand palmed her cheek, stroking her face with trembling fingers. "Good. You okay?"

She nodded, lifting one hand to her forehead. The baseball cap was in place, but beneath the band, her head hurt. She pulled off the hat, letting her hair tumble free, and checked the adhesive bandage covering the gash at her hairline. It was still in place.

"Did I hit my head?" she asked.

"You went headfirst into the window, but the bill of the cap stopped you from smashing your face." He curved his hand beneath her chin, lifting her face to look at her forehead. "Don't see any blood seeping through the bandage. You dodged a bullet."

"How long was I out of it that time?" She looked around them, trying to regain her bearings. They were parked on the shoulder of the road, surrounded primarily by woods. It was the mountain road leading up to the cabins that dotted the mountainside. The town was behind them now, no longer visible through the trees.

"Just a minute or two." Wade leaned down and picked up the cell phone sitting between her feet.

She eyed it warily, realizing that whatever had triggered her flashback must have been on that video. Cautiously, she tried to remember the images she'd seen when she hit the play button.

The interior of the shop, a familiar, pleasant sight. Her mouth watered, even now, at the memory of the display case full of chocolate candies. Wade had moved the phone slowly around the shop interior, taking in the cross-stitched samplers hanging on the wall and the smiling face of the college-aged counter clerk.

There had been customers. Tourists, mostly, dressed in casual clothing, milling around the display cases in search of candy delights they could eat, guilt free, because they were on vacation.

And then the camera had panned toward the far wall—

"Let me take a look at the video again," she said, holding out her hand.

Wade eyed her warily. "Not sure that's a good idea."

She could hardly blame him for his hesitation. She buckled her seat belt, pulling it tight, and held out her hand again. "Please?"

He slowly released his breath and handed her the phone. She pushed the play button and watched the video run through the cycle again. Entranceway, candy counter, yummy chocolates, pretty counter clerk—there. Wade was telling the story of the fishing trip and the girlfriend stuck home working as he swung the camera toward the side wall.

A man stood by the preboxed chocolates, pretending to be considering his options. From the back, he looked ordinary enough, just another tourist dressed in khaki chinos and a light blue golf shirt. But when he turned toward Wade, he froze a second, then quickly turned his head away.

But not soon enough.

She rewound and hit Pause when the man's face turned fully toward her. He wore a fishing hat adorned with tied flies, but it rode high enough to reveal an ordinary face, wide brow, flat cheekbones, thin mouth and square chin. There was nothing remarkable about him at all, but Annie recognized him nevertheless.

She'd seen his face before, in the front room of her father's mountain cabin. He'd been waiting for them just inside when they returned from breakfast on the second morning of their vacation.

He hadn't been alone.

"You recognize him?" Wade asked carefully, his voice breaking her concentration, making her jump.

She released a bitter chuckle. "He's one of the people who took us from the cabin."

"You remember?"

She nodded, a shudder rippling down her back. "Not all the details, but I know he was there. There were others, too. I don't remember anything about them, just that they were there."

"Still, that's great. That's amazing." He put his hand on her shoulder, the touch careful. Tentative.

But she found the touch bracing. As he started to move his hand away, she covered his fingers with hers, holding his hand in place. "Thank you."

"For what?"

"You took a big risk coming here with me. I know you didn't have to."

He gave her shoulder a squeeze and tugged his hand gently from her grasp. "Let's see if I can catch a still from this and email it back to Gossamer Ridge."

"Won't that reveal our whereabouts? Since your

brother thinks someone's keeping a close eye on your family, I mean."

"It'll go to Luke first. He can forward it to Jesse. Or take it to my cousin Aaron and let him see if we can get an ID on this guy."

She was afraid to hope anything helpful could come from identifying the man in the video. Even if they established that he was somehow connected to the S.S.U., it would only be confirmation of what they already believed.

She might not remember exactly what had happened to her family, but she knew, gut deep, that the S.S.U. was somehow involved.

"Okay, sent." Wade pocketed the phone and buckled his seat belt, turning the key in the ignition. The Ram roared to life. "I don't think we need to head up the mountain just yet, do you?"

She knew what he was asking. "You don't trust me not to zone out on you again."

"I just think one zone out is enough for one day. Why don't we find a motel next town over and settle down for the night?"

She ran her finger along the strap of the seat belt, a new thought occurring to her. They hadn't taken time to consider all the ramifications of their precipitous flight east while they were eating up highway to put distance between themselves and the people back in Chickasaw County who were looking for Annie. But there was something neither of them had considered.

"I think we should get one room," Wade said.

Okay, maybe he *had* considered it.

"Because you might have another flashback," he added quickly, meeting her sidelong gaze.

"Right."

It was the only reasonable option. For one thing, she wasn't sure how safe either of them would be stuck in a strange room alone, separated from the only support either of them had. And if she were to have another flashback and wander off in her altered state, God only knew where she'd end up before she came back to her senses.

"Or we could go back to Alabama and let my cousin put you in protective custody," Wade added quietly.

She looked over at him. He was gazing forward, into the woods that stretched out ahead of them on the winding road up the mountain, his profile set and impossible to read. "Is that what you'd rather I do? I mean, like I said, it's asking a lot of you—"

He shot her a quick, fierce look. "I don't know where you'd be safer. That's the only thing that matters."

"I'd be safer with you." The words spilled from her lips, thoughtless and unfiltered. But sure. Utterly sure.

His eyes blazed back at her. "Okay, then. Let's find a cheap motel and settle in for the night."

THE MOUNTAIN VIEW LODGE in Samsonville, about twenty minutes north of Pea Hollow, wasn't nearly as scenic as its name would suggest. Wade found the clerk more than willing to take cash—with a generous tip—rather than a credit card to pay for the night's stay. He drove the truck around and hurried Annie inside, careful to get her quickly out of sight of any nosy fellow travelers in nearby rooms.

There were two beds, neither of them particularly inviting, but Annie didn't seem inclined to be picky. She dropped onto the nearest bed and slumped forward, her elbows resting on her knees. "This running for your life stuff? Not as exciting as it looks on TV."

He plucked his cap off her head, making her look up at him. "Tell me the truth. How are you feeling? How's the head?"

"Okay," she said. She sounded truthful enough. "I could use a hot shower, though."

"Me, too." The long drive had been hell on his bad right knee. A hot shower might loosen up the aching muscles.

She cocked her head. "You go first. And don't use up the hot water."

"You sure?"

She nodded, grabbing the paper bag he'd dropped

on the bed next to her. "I'll be here examining the pistachio clusters." She waggled her eyebrows, making him grin.

He showered quickly and changed into a clean pair of jeans and a faded olive drab T-shirt from his Marine Corps days. The hot water had eased some of the pain in his knee, but his limp was still far more pronounced than he liked as he hobbled his way back to the main room.

"The beds are remarkably clean," Annie commented from her supine position on the far bed, her words garbled by the pistachio cluster she was chewing. "Don't suppose they have cable?"

Wade sat on the opposite bed. "Don't ruin your dinner." They'd stopped at a fast food restaurant a quarter mile back, grabbing burgers and soft drinks to supplement the small stash of packaged food Wade had shoved into his duffel bag.

She wrinkled her nose and sat up, putting the bag of candy aside. She nodded at his knee, which he'd begun to rub absentmindedly. "Still hurts?"

"Like a son of a bitch," he admitted.

She pushed off the bed and crossed to sit next to him. "My dad busted his knee when I was still in high school. He was terrified it would kill his career—pilots with bad limbs don't go very far. I used to help him with his home physical therapy. I learned a lot." She met Wade's gaze, a question in her warm caramel eyes.

Feeling suddenly helpless to deny her anything, he gave a little nod.

She curved her hand over his bum knee, her fingers gently probing the swollen joint. "Nerve damage?"

"Some," he admitted, feeling flushed and unnerved.

"Torn muscles," she said, her fingers sliding over the malformed muscles where the bullet had torn through flesh and bone. "Ouch."

"Yeah." Clinical though her examination might be, it was having a decidedly non-clinical effect on his body. Though he struggled not to let it show, his blood sang in his veins with each gentle touch, his body growing fiery hot with sexual awareness. If her fingers moved any farther up his leg, he might not be able to hide his reaction from her at all.

She dropped her hand away from his knee and slowly lifted her face, answering fire blazing in her eyes. "What are we doing?" she whispered, leaning perilously close.

"I don't know," he admitted, unable to move away. She was so close he could feel the heat of her skin radiating against his. Her breath washed over him, sweet from the candy and smoldering hot with the same desire that burned behind her eyes.

He had to taste her, sample the molten sweetness himself.

She curled her hand in the collar of his shirt,

twisting the cotton to pull him closer. He pressed his mouth to hers, his breath spilling from his lungs in a heated rush.

Sweet and salty. Blistering hot and smoky dark. As her hands slid around his neck, he wrapped his arms around her waist and dragged her closer, needing to feel her body pressed hot and firm against his.

She made a sound deep in her throat, her fingers clawing into his back. Suddenly, her body went rigid against his, and the sound in her throat rose in a cry.

He jerked away from her as she slammed her hands hard against his shoulders, a rat-a-tat of terror. She scrambled away from him, staring back at him through sightless eyes.

She was gone again.

# Chapter Eight

The room was dark and smelled of sweat and fear.

Her sweat. Her fear.

When the door opened with a rattle of metal on metal, Annie jerked out of her stupor of despair, going rigid with dreadful anticipation.

Visits over the past few days had been sporadically spaced, chosen, she was certain, to maximize her anxiety. Give her time to shake and shiver in fear and despair, waiting for the next time he came.

Not the same man every time. Though they kept her almost entirely in the dark when they entered the room, she could still differentiate them through their voices, both the timbre and the accent. One of them was from Louisiana, with a broad bayou drawl that did nothing to soften the cruelty of his taunts. Another was from somewhere up north. He'd disappeared early on, after the first week. There was a third man, the one who wielded the needles. She hated him and his flat, neutral accent.

There was a fourth man as well. He was black,

with a light urban southern accent, though that wasn't the only thing that distinguished him from the others. His tone was almost gentle. Relatively kind. He wasn't a taunter. He just brought her food and backed out of the room in an economy of movement and speech. She hadn't seen him in a while, either.

She'd begun to miss him dreadfully.

The light came on, a flashlight, shining straight into her eyes. Her pupils contracted painfully and her eyelids tried to slam shut. The light moved closer, sliced more painfully into her eyes.

"Hungry?" This voice belonged to the man from Louisiana. Fear crept up her spine like an army of spiders, tightening muscles and turning her insides to liquid.

"I want to see my father." She didn't know why she said it yet again. She knew her tiny act of defiance would earn her greater punishment, but she feared that if she didn't keep asking that one question every time someone walked into her cell, she'd lose herself completely to her terror. Then it wouldn't matter if she ever escaped at all.

"You know that's not going to happen, beautiful." His voice was close, his breath hot on her cheek. She could see him now, even though he kept the light in her eyes. He was shadowy and indistinct, but at least she could see his eyes, glittering in the reflected beam of the flashlight.

"You can't keep me here forever."

"No. I don't think that's in the plan, sweetheart." He touched her neck, sliding one finger downward, across her ever more prominent collarbone. They hadn't starved her at all, but she could find no appetite for anything more than the bare minimum she had to eat to subsist.

Her skin crawled where he touched her, quivering beneath his fingers. Maybe he could even feel her shudders, because he just laughed. "The rules are, look, don't touch."

"What do you call torturing me?" she spat back at him, her skin still tingling from the last go they'd had at her with the needle. She wasn't sure what they were injecting into her, but it burned like crazy. They didn't allow her a lot of light even when they weren't around, so she hadn't gotten a very good look at the marks the needles had left in her skin.

"There's different kinds of touching, baby girl." His growl held a definite sexual tone. His breath was hotter, closer. She could smell a faint remnant of coffee and a cool, sharp rush of wintergreen mint.

"I want to see my father." She repeated the words like a prayer, as if they could somehow keep her from going completely over the edge into insanity.

His voice lowered to a purr. "Maybe I could do something about that, if you did something for me."

She heard the scrape of a zipper, and her whole body contracted with revulsion.

Suddenly the door opened, spilling light into the scene. A tall, dark silhouette stood in the doorway, broad-shouldered and powerful. "Out," he said.

The darkness around her fractured into soft, waning daylight.

It took a second to reorient herself. She wasn't strapped to a wall in a dark, dank room. Instead, she sat on a bed, held upright by a pair of strong, warm arms. She twisted free of those arms, needing space and distance. Needing to feel her own autonomy.

She ended up backing into another bed and sat with a thud. Wade Cooper sat facing her on the opposite bed, his dark eyes wary.

"Annie?"

"I'm okay," she said. And she was. Even the crawling revulsion and bone-rattling fear from the dream had seeped quickly away, swallowed by reality.

More important, she remembered the flashback this time.

All of it. The sensory elements—dark room, hard wall, tight restraints. The smell of coffee and mint on her captor's breath. The glitter of his eyes in the low light. Even the sound of his voice.

"The man from the candy shop," she said aloud. "He was definitely one of my captors."

"We figured that."

"And I don't think they raped me," she added, relief fluttering in her belly. "He said they had a 'look, don't touch' policy with me." She grimaced. "But he wasn't happy about that rule."

"You remember the flashback this time?" He looked surprised.

She nodded. "I do. It's not a confabulation. It's a memory. It's too clear, too detailed to be anything else."

"Do you remember where you were?"

"Just that it was a small room. No windows—they kept me in the dark as much as possible. I think maybe to protect them more than to punish me." She wasn't sure why she thought that to be the case, but it just felt right. "They kept me chained to the wall. I didn't have much room to move at all."

"Did they starve you?"

She shook her head. "Three meals a day." She was sure of that, too, though she didn't have a distinct memory of eating any of those meals.

"Do you remember everything?"

"No," she admitted. "It's kind of strange—I remember everything about that moment, that memory. Anything I knew about my experience as a captive to that point, I remember. But I don't remember how I got there or how I got away."

"You remembered stowing away on a truck before, right?"

She nodded. "I think it was some sort of trailer truck. Enclosed."

"Do you remember what was inside the truck?"

She tried to picture it, to get past that vague sensation of being enclosed and traveling, but she couldn't push past the invisible wall between herself and the memory. "No."

"That's okay. You remembered a lot more this time. And you retained it. That's new, isn't it?"

"Yes." She looked across the narrow space between them, taking in his hopeful look. He really wanted her to remember, she realized. But for her own sake? Or for his family's investigation?

And where did that kiss figure in?

His eyes narrowed as he noticed her sudden scrutiny. "Are you remembering something else?"

"You kissed me."

He actually blushed a little, his dark eyes softening. "Yeah. Though, technically, I think it was sort of a joint effort."

She managed a smile. "Fair enough."

His answering smile faded quickly. "Is that what triggered the flashback?"

"I guess it was," she conceded.

"That bad?" He said it lightly, but she heard a sliver of vulnerability behind the words.

"No." She wasn't sure how to explain what she thought might be behind the correlation, but he'd been good to her so far. He deserved the effort. "I think maybe it had more to do with the way I was feeling."

"Repulsed?"

"No." She made a face at him. "Vulnerable."

"Oh."

"I felt out of control, and I guess that's what really triggered it." She looked down at her hands, noticing for the first time how short and ragged her nails were. She'd always taken care with her manicure, growing her nails long and keeping them neat and polished as befit a professional woman, mostly because as an awkward teenager, she'd had a bad habit of chewing them to nubs.

She rolled her hands into fists, hiding her nails from herself. "It was a nice kiss."

"Not sure how you'd know," he murmured. "You flashed back pretty fast there."

"I still remember the start," she said. "It was nice...."

"But?"

She met his questioning gaze. "But I don't think it should happen again. Not right now." Maybe not ever.

"Okay."

She slanted a look at him, unexpectedly hurt by his glib agreement. "Not even a token protest, just for my self-esteem?"

He grinned at her, and she felt a flutter of regret that she'd just closed the door on another kiss.

He *was* awfully cute, especially when he grinned. And distracting herself from her boatload of worries with another round of snogging with the cowboy Marine was more tempting than she expected.

"Tell you what," he said, still smiling. "When we get your folks back and you're ready to look at life from a more normal viewpoint, if you're inclined to make out with a gimpy old Marine, you know where to find me."

She smiled back at him, trying to imagine what it would be like to have her life back to normal. Was that even going to be possible, after what she and her parents had been through?

Her smile faded as she remembered something else. Not from her most recent flashback but from the one before. She remembered the sound of her father's voice, his tone low and urgent. She felt a black rush of terror as the words rang in her head, suddenly certain they'd been spoken in a rush as the world spun out of control around them.

*If you get out of here, find Marsh.*

"Annie?"

"I'm not flashing back," she said, looking up at him.

"You seemed a little distant."

*Find Marsh.* That's why she'd gone to the lake house.

Her father had told her if she got away from their

captors, she had to go find General Marsh. And he'd also told her to protect the code.

But what code?

Wade's cell phone rang, the loud trill sending a jolt of electricity through Annie's nervous system. She snapped her gaze up to meet his and found him staring back at her, his brow furrowed. He answered the phone. "Yeah?"

He listened for a moment. "Hold on, let me put this on speaker." He pushed a button. "Go ahead."

Luke Cooper's deep voice came over the staticky line. "As I was saying, we have an ID on the guy in the candy shop. Rick dropped by the stable to take a look at the video and he says it's a guy named Toby Lavelle."

The name meant nothing to Annie, but Wade's expression darkened. "Isn't that the gunrunner Scanlon came across in Bolen Bluff back in April?"

"One and the same. Former MacLear agent, apparently did black ops stuff with the Special Services Unit before the company fell. Rick says he's a nasty son of a bitch—you'll want to stay well clear."

Wade met Annie's gaze. "Yeah, I think we figured that out already."

"How are y'all holding up?"

"Okay for now," Wade said carefully, but he shot a questioning look at Annie.

She nodded quickly, though the rush of information swamping her at the moment—from Luke

Cooper's call to her own influx of disjointed memories— had her feeling anything but okay.

"Don't want to stay on the line too long," Wade said.

"Stay in touch," Luke said.

"Will do." Wade hung up the phone and slipped it back into his pocket, his gaze still tangling with Annie's. "Why don't you go ahead and take your shower? I'll get the burgers out and we can eat."

A shower sounded like a wonderful idea, though she was beginning to wonder how much longer her shaking legs could bear her weight. She showered as quickly as she could and dried off quickly, even as her legs threatened to give way beneath her.

She made it into a clean pair of jeans and a long-sleeved T-shirt before her legs gave out, and she sank down to the floor in front of the sink.

Hot tears leaked from her eyes. She batted at them with her knuckles, but they kept coming, burning her eyes. A soft sob escaped her throat and she clamped her mouth shut to keep any more from getting free. But her body shook with each aborted sob, each swallowed wail of despair.

How had her life turned so utterly, irrevocably upside down? Her mind—the one attribute she'd always prized most highly—had betrayed her, keeping dark and dangerous secrets from her in a cruel game of hide-and-seek. Her body, which she'd worked hard to keep strong and fit, had wasted into this fragile shell that couldn't even hold her upright long enough to take a quick shower.

Nothing made sense. Nothing seemed familiar in this upended world in which she had awakened not twenty-four hours ago.

*Give yourself time.* The voice she heard in her mind was her mother's, gentle and understanding as always. Guileless and sweet. Cathy Harlowe was the kindest person Annie knew, and she'd tried all her life to balance the fiery drive she'd inherited from her ambitious father with the goodness of her mother.

Another sob tore through her, bursting past the tight clench of her jaw. Where was her mother now? What had those bastards done to her? Of all the people in the world, Annie could think of no one who less deserved to be tormented and abused.

A soft rap on the bathroom door sent her scuttling backward, instinctively seeking the protection of the sink. It took a second for her hypervigilant brain to process the fact that it was almost certainly Wade Cooper on the other side of the door. And if she didn't answer him quickly, he'd come inside and witness her meltdown.

She tried to speak, but her aching throat closed. And then it was too late. Wade opened the door and stuck his head inside.

His dark gaze met hers, and she looked away, humiliated.

After a moment, he entered the bathroom, and she heard the door close behind him. It seemed an odd thing to do, shutting them in when there was no one else in the motel room, but she found the extra seclusion strangely comforting.

Wade sat down next to her on the floor, careful not to touch her. "Are you hurt?"

She shook her head, still not looking at him. "Just having a moment."

"Ah." He was quiet for a few seconds, then spoke in a lowered voice. "I fell flat on my butt the first time I tried to take a bath alone after my injury. I was stark naked in the bathroom and completely unable to get back up. And the only person in the house at the time was my cousin Hannah, who'd dropped by to check on me."

She winced at the picture he painted.

"You think it was bad for me, think about poor Hannah. But she's a Cooper, so she just hauled my sorry naked butt up and lectured me about trying to go too fast. Healing takes time."

"And sometimes it never happens," she replied, her voice tight with tears. "Sometimes, things can't be fixed."

He rubbed his bad knee. "That's true. But they can usually be endured, if you just give yourself a break."

"If I could just remember what happened—"

"It's been only a day since I found you. Not even

that long. You can't expect it all to come flooding back at once. I'm not even sure your brain could handle that kind of onslaught."

She looked at him then. "What I know could save my family if I could just remember it."

"You've already remembered some things, haven't you?"

She looked away again. She'd remembered more than she'd told him.

"I've been thinking," he said when she didn't respond. "I don't think it's a good idea for us to stick around here with that S.S.U. guy hanging around. He may be looking for you, figuring you'd show back up to the place where you last saw your folks."

Part of her agreed with him utterly, the quivering, cowering part of her sitting here hiding under a motel room sink. But that wasn't who she was. That part of her wasn't supposed to call the shots in Annie Harlowe's life.

She had a backbone, too. And she still remembered how to use it.

Annie scooted out from under the sink and pushed to her feet, surprised and pleased to find that her legs weren't shaking any longer. "I'm not done here," she said, looking down at him.

He gazed up at her. "Okay." He put his hands down beside him and tried to push to his feet, but he seemed to be having difficulty. Finally, he flushed dark red and dropped his head to his chest.

"Damn it. I knew better than to get down here on the floor."

Annie reached her hand down to him. He looked at her hand, then at her. Suddenly, he grinned and she felt the same strong tug of attraction that had landed her in a lip-lock with him just a short time earlier. But she didn't draw back her hand when he reached for it, closing her fingers around his to give him leverage to maneuver himself up.

He stumbled a little when he got to his feet, his weight driving her backward against the bathroom door. She felt a flood of heat run straight to her core as his hard body flattened against hers for a long, breathless moment.

His face was so close it made her dizzy to try to look into his dark, deep eyes. Eyes fluttering shut, she grabbed the fabric of his T-shirt in the fist of one hand, swallowing a groan of need.

*Don't kiss me again*, she thought. *I don't know if I can take it if you kiss me again.*

Wade flattened his palms against the door on either side of her head and pushed himself backward, robbing her of his heat. She swallowed another groan, this time of disappointment.

"Sorry," he murmured.

She opened her eyes and found him looking back at her, his gaze brimming with questions.

She pulled herself together, lifting her chin and straightening her back. "No harm done." She opened the bathroom door and slipped outside, leaving him to follow.

On the table near the window, he'd laid out their dinner—two hamburgers, still wrapped in foil in a probably futile attempt to keep them warm. Their drinks were sweating condensation onto the laminate tabletop.

She sat, leaving Wade to take the opposite chair. "Thank you."

"For what?"

"For dinner." She slanted a look at him and smiled. "And for getting down on the floor with me, even though you knew you might have trouble getting back up."

"Not one of my finer moments." He focused his attention on unwrapping his hamburger.

"On the contrary."

He glanced up at her. "You like your men gimpy and stupid?"

She sighed. "Is that really how you see yourself?"

He shook his head. "I still think of myself as unimpaired. Maybe that's my problem. I'm not being realistic."

She had a feeling his problem was actually the opposite. She'd seen him move when they were in a hurry. He'd been limping along at first, while pushing her chair, but he'd had no trouble running through the tunnel once they realized there were people coming up fast behind them. And while they'd been rushing around preparing to leave Gossamer Ridge, he'd shown little sign of his injury at all, his limp almost imperceptible.

She supposed it was a realization he was going to have to come to on his own, however. As long as he felt crippled, he was.

In the meantime, she'd come to a realization of her own, one she was pretty sure Wade wasn't going to want to hear. She wasn't especially happy about the decision she'd made herself, given how easily she slipped into her weird flashback states.

But every second that passed put her parents in graver danger. She didn't have time to recover before she put her neck on the line for them.

"There's something I've decided," she said aloud.

Wade's wary expression made her stomach knot. "What is it?"

"Well, for one thing, I think we stick around here another night."

His eyes narrowed. "Not a good idea."

"Maybe not, but it's my best chance to remember what happened the night my parents and I were taken." She folded the wrapper over her half-eaten hamburger, her gut rolling too much to consider eating anything more. "I've already remembered more since we've been here than I did back in Gossamer Ridge. I think I can remember more."

"The triggers are too dangerous. We know there's at least one S.S.U. thug out there looking for you."

"It can't be helped."

Wade's lips pressed to a thin line before he spoke. "What exactly do you have in mind?"

She swallowed her reluctance and blurted out her plan. "Tomorrow night, we're going inside my family's vacation cabin."

## Chapter Nine

"This is the craziest damned idea you've come up with yet," Wade breathed, keeping his gaze pinned to the moonlit cabin thirty yards ahead.

"Duly noted, for the hundredth time," Annie murmured back, shooting him a weary look. She hadn't wanted to hear his objections, batting them all away with the stubborn determination of a single-minded soldier on a dangerous but necessary mission.

She needed to do this. And as much as he hated it, he had to let her. Her family was in danger, and he knew if the situation were reversed, he'd crawl through a swamp full of hungry alligators to help his own family.

"There's no movement anywhere around the cabin," she whispered as the silence of the woods stretched around them. Even the animals and birds were quiet, as if aware of intruders in their peaceful midst.

"There could be people stationed inside."

She shook her head. "The authorities released the cabin as a crime scene over a week ago. I read it in the articles online."

With little else to do but hole up in the motel room and wait for nightfall, Annie had spent a large portion of the day on Wade's laptop, combing the internet for news articles about her family's disappearance. She'd hoped it might spark more memories, but all it had seemed to do was make her angrier and more determined than ever to get to the bottom of what had happened to them here in this secluded mountain cabin nearly four weeks ago.

"I wasn't talking about the cops," Wade said flatly.

She glanced at him, her eyes gleaming in the pale moonlight seeping through the thinning trees overhead. The warmer weather of early September was starting to give way to cooler temperatures as the month progressed, especially here in the north Georgia mountains, dropping the temperatures into the low sixties at night. Fall was coming, and winter not far behind.

Wade prayed it wouldn't take that long to find Annie's family. Based on what she'd shared of her time in captivity, the conditions had been primitive at best. If the temperature dropped below freezing—

"Let's just do it," Annie said, tugging on the sleeve of his denim jacket. "There's nobody in there, but if we wait around much longer—"

"Okay." She was right. Every minute they waited could be a minute wasted. Wade didn't see any obvious signs that there were people hiding inside the cabin. But just because they weren't there at the moment didn't mean they wouldn't show up sooner or later. If they were looking for Annie, the cabin would be an obvious place to look.

"I don't know if you know much about moving with stealth," Wade murmured, "but if you do, use it." He struck out ahead of her, painfully conscious of his bad knee. It wasn't hurting at the moment, despite the trek up the mountain from where he'd hidden the truck. But it still didn't feel right. It felt unreliable, as if it might turn on him in an instant.

He tried to drive that thought from his mind as he edged forward through the trees, coming ever closer to the narrow clearing around the cabin. When the trees thinned out to nothing, he paused and turned to look at Annie. "Still not too late to turn back."

The glare she sent his way would have knocked over a less sturdy man. He took a deep breath and started to step out into the clearing when an obvious question, one he should have asked before he stepped foot out of the motel room, occurred to him. "Do you have a key?"

Annie shook her head. "But I know where to find one."

ANNIE AND HER PARENTS had all kept keys to the cabin on their key rings. It wasn't a rental place, like so many cabins in the area, but property her father had bought by saving money over the years so that the family would have a place of refuge from the pressures of his demanding job. He'd wanted any of them to be able to escape there at any time, without worrying about whether the property was otherwise occupied. They used it enough that it was worth the upkeep, whether it was a weekend trip for her and her mother or, when Annie had been a little younger, a fun getaway for her and her college friends.

Even though they all had keys, her father had hidden a spare near the cabin, not in any of the obvious places, like under a window sill or in a flowerpot, but tucked into the knothole of a tree stump about ten yards east of the house. A tornado had taken the top of the tree down years ago, but the trunk was solid and had withstood hundreds of storms since.

Praying no creepy, crawly creature had made its home in the knothole since the last time she'd had to use the hidden key, Annie stuck her finger inside and felt the cool metal of the small key box that protected the key from the elements.

Time and moisture had made the little box rust, but it creaked open and revealed the key.

"Clever," Wade murmured over her shoulder.

"You realize now that I've shown you the secret hiding place, I have to kill you."

He grinned at her, though his cheek twitched a bit. He didn't like being out in the open so long.

Neither did she.

They hurried up the front porch of the cabin and used the key on the lock. The door made a low creaking noise that sent her heart racing double time. She closed the door behind them, and they paused in the middle of the entranceway, listening with hushed anxiety for any noise that might reveal they were not alone.

After a moment, Wade broke the silence with a soft snick of his flashlight. What Annie saw in the narrow beam of light playing across the cabin's front room made her gasp.

The place had been turned upside down. Cabinet drawers opened, furniture cushions upended. A film of fingerprint powder lay across every available surface. It hadn't been like this when the men had taken her and her parents out of here.

She gave a small start at the unexpected memory.

"What?" Wade whispered.

"I remember looking back at this room as they were dragging me out of here, and it looked so normal at the time. They'd come in fast, overpowered us. We didn't even have time to fight, so we didn't cause much of a mess."

She felt Wade's hand close over her shoulder. "You remember it?" he asked. "Not a flashback?"

Despite the creeping sensation of danger closing in on all sides, she couldn't hold back a smile. "I remember it. Just that one moment, looking back at the cabin and wondering if anyone would ever know what happened to us."

The hand on her shoulder squeezed lightly. "I guess the mess came from the police."

Clearly.

"Be careful not to disturb anything," Wade added.

Annie wasn't sure how they were supposed to navigate this mess without moving anything, but she couldn't argue with him.

"What do you hope to find here?" Wade asked quietly as they moved deeper into the cabin, navigating by the beam of his flashlight.

"Answers," she replied, knowing she was being frustratingly vague.

Where had she been when the intruders struck? She thought back to all the times she and her parents had come to stay here. When it had been just her and her mom, they'd spent a lot of time outside on the porch, rocking in the twin pine rockers and catching up on their lives apart. When her dad was around, they often gathered in the kitchen to prepare meals together, since her father was a frustrated chef at heart. Or if her mother was napping or doing something elsewhere, sometimes Annie and her father retired into his small study, where he kept his vacation books, as he called them.

She gravitated there, drawn by happy memories of her father's favorite place in the cabin. His job had taken up so much of his time that the simple freedom to sit in the big leather armchair in the corner and read a good novel or one of the biographies he loved to devour was a rare luxury.

She could picture him there, one leg crossed over the other, his black horn-rimmed reading glasses perched low on his nose as he read. The chair was now dusty with fingerprint powder. The chair opposite, a smaller armchair with rust-colored canvas upholstery, had been left undusted, probably since the nubby fabric wasn't likely to take prints.

"You want to stick around here a little while?" Wade asked, his quiet voice making her whole body jerk.

"Yeah. Is that okay?"

"Sure. But I think I'll go look around the rest of the cabin." He held out his flashlight to her.

"Won't you need it?"

"I have a spare." He pulled another flashlight from his pocket, a smaller penlight, and flicked it on. The beam was less powerful, but she supposed it would serve his purposes.

She took the flashlight he offered, realizing only after he left that he probably understood her reluctance to stay in a dark place alone. He could have left her the smaller light, given that she was about to sit still in a room while he was wandering about, but he knew she'd feel better with the stronger source of light to drive away the shadows around her.

A good man, Wade Cooper.

She double-checked the rust armchair to be sure that it was powder-free and sat, staring at the leather chair that sat opposite. She pictured her father there, saw his dark eyes flicker up to meet hers.

*Finished with the hen party?* he had teased her the last time she'd sat across from him in this chair. His voice was a low, drawling rumble in her mind, clear and fresh in her memory.

It had happened the day she'd arrived at the Chattanooga airport, she realized. He and her mother had picked her up and conveyed her back here in her father's big, silver Ford Expedition, her mother chatting happily for the entire hour's drive.

It had been a long time since they'd had time to chat, she remembered, because she'd been working hard on that lead about the Barton Reid case. There were rumors, bordering on educated guesses, that despite how high Barton Reid had ranked at the State Department, people even higher ranked than he were probably involved in the conspiracy to manipulate global events to suit their purposes.

The deeper she'd investigated, the more she'd hit walls. Her parents' invitation to join them for a week's vacation in the mountains had come at the perfect time. She'd been happy to put D.C. and her investigation on the back burner for a little while, hoping the time and distance might give her a new perspective on the case.

Instead, it had turned her world upside down.

She remembered, she realized. She remembered spotting her parents at the airport and waving them over. Her father had insisted on carrying her suitcase, while her mother had hooked her arm through Annie's and started her usual gentle interrogation about Annie's love life.

Which had been, for most of the last year, pretty arid.

After a while, she and her mother had exhausted the usual topics of conversation, and while Cathy had gone to take a shower before bedtime, she'd come here to the study to spend a little time with her father.

He hadn't been reading a book this time, she remembered. Instead, he'd been sitting here, staring out the window, his hands steepled under his chin.

She'd smiled at his joke about the hen party, knowing that he adored her mother precisely because of her gentle, social spirit, a fine foil for his own quiet, reserved personality. But his return smile had faded quickly, and she remembered a twisting sensation in her gut, as if she knew he had something deadly serious to tell her.

She'd been afraid he was going to tell her that he or her mother was ill. Cancer, maybe. Or, given their advancing ages, perhaps the early onset of Alzheimer's. She'd sat across from him, bracing herself for whatever had put that grim expression on his usually placid face.

"I have to go to Nightshade Island later this week, to see Lydia."

Nightshade Island didn't ring any bells for her, but the name Lydia did. Lydia Ross was the widow of one of her father's oldest, closest friends. General Edward Ross had been, along with her father and Marine Corps General Baxter Marsh, the three generals heading up the peacekeeping mission in Kaziristan. Following the al Adar uprising in that country that had begun with a siege on the U.S. and British embassies in the capital city of Tablis, the three generals had mapped out a strategy to support the Kaziri government in reestablishing and maintaining order in the volatile country.

The mission was still ongoing, especially as Kaziristan prepared for their first democratic election since the siege, but all three of the generals had been relieved of duty a year earlier with the changing of the guard at the Department of Defense.

At the age of sixty-seven, her father had decided to take retirement, a choice that had surprised her at the time, given how much he'd loved his Air Force career. But as he continued telling her about his plans for the next week, his decision made a horrible sort of sense.

"I believe Edward was murdered to keep him from sharing the evidence we were gathering against Barton Reid and our suspicions about a higher-reaching conspiracy."

"Conspiracy to do what?" she'd asked, her gut twisting as she realized that the death of one of them made the death of all three of them the obvious goal of whoever had killed General Ross.

Was her father in danger as well? Was General Marsh?

"We're not sure," her father admitted. "We only know who we think may be involved and some of the activities they've been involved in. Edward wrote all of it down in a journal, including the evidence that the three of us found independently. I need to protect that journal."

"What if the people who killed him took it?"

"I've spoken to his wife. There've been no breaches on the island, so it should be safe for now. Besides, I'm fairly sure the people who arranged his car crash don't know about the journal, or they'd never have killed him."

"I'm not sure I follow," she'd admitted.

"The information was written in a complex code Edward created while we were still in Kaziristan. We didn't want to risk the kind of internal leaks that compromised so many other missions. " Her father had shot her an apologetic look. "No offense, darling, but the press can be vultures, and there are too many young soldiers holding grudges or radical ideas about war and freedom to be entrusted with high-level communications in a war zone. You remember what happened with those data leaks—"

She remembered. "You know I didn't agree with that."

"Of course I know that. You're my daughter." He smiled with pride. "You understand the importance of operational secrecy. You know people die if the wrong people learn the wrong information."

It had always been a difficult balance, choosing between the natural desire for absolute transparency and the necessary secrecy involved in combat, a fine line she'd walked her entire career. "So General Ross created a code?"

"A tri-layered code. Each of us possess a piece. The journal can't be decoded without all three parts."

"And now General Ross has died, and with him part of the code?"

"No. Each of us agreed to entrust the code to someone else, in case anything happened to us."

She'd felt a flutter of fear, realizing just how much danger he must be in to tell her even this much of his secret. "You're afraid something's going to happen to you, just like it happened to General Ross."

He'd reached across the space between them and caught her hand. "I'm going to do all I can to avoid that possibility. But the problem is, I haven't yet entrusted the code to anyone else."

She looked at him, seeing in his eyes why he'd really asked her to join them here at the cabin. "Dad—"

He'd squeezed her hand. "I trust you. I know you will protect it with your life."

She'd listened in fearful silence as he'd explained the parameters of his layer of the code. It was deceptively simple, and with a few repetitions, she was able to commit the code to memory.

"Protect it, darling," her father had said, his voice deep and urgent.

*Protect the code.*

She remembered.

She pressed her hand over her mouth, feeling sick. It had been the next morning when she and her parents had returned from breakfast to an ambush. Annie remembered the look on her father's face as he tried to fight off the attackers, to protect her and her mother from their intentions.

And then, she realized with a whimper of frustration, her memory disappeared into a deep, black void.

"Annie!"

Wade's harsh whisper, close behind her, sent a jolt through her nervous system. Trembling all over, she turned to look at him. He gazed back at her, his eyes fathomless in the beam of her flashlight.

"Shut down your light," he whispered.

Then she heard it. The sound of a vehicle coming up the road, the rumble of its engine soft but unmistakable.

Someone was coming to the cabin.

## Chapter Ten

He should never have agreed to come here, Wade thought as he followed Annie through the darkened cabin toward the back exit, especially given her recent bouts with debilitating flashbacks. But after her first shaky reaction, she'd responded with surprising confidence, extinguishing the flashlight and leading the way toward the back.

They reached the back door before the car engine died at the front of the cabin. Annie opened the door and slipped outside, grabbing his arm to pull him out behind her. They closed the door quietly, the click of the latch engaging camouflaged by the sound of footsteps ringing on the front porch steps of the cabin.

Annie slipped the key in the lock and twisted it. "I didn't lock the front door behind us," she whispered, her brow furrowed.

"I locked it when I heard the car coming," he whispered back. He held up his hands to show her he'd donned a pair of thin leather gloves. "No prints."

She shot him a look of relief. There might have been a little admiration in her expression as well, though he supposed he could be indulging in a bit of wishful thinking.

He didn't have time for wishful thinking.

"Come on." Annie tightened her fingers around his. She led him into the tree line at the back of the cabin until he could barely see the building through the thick palisade of tree trunks and low-hanging limbs.

"Now we can't see what they're doing," Wade murmured.

"Just a minute." She kept moving, tugging him with her, until they reached four pine trees lined up side by side like sentries standing guard. Overhead, their boughs tangled inextricably, as if they were holding hands in a giant game of Red Rover. But between their wide, rough trunks, Wade could see the cabin.

"We called them the four sisters," Annie whispered. "Mom and I. Dad said we were being fanciful."

Wade peered through the darkness at the cabin. From this vantage point, he could see the porch and the side window of the large front room.

Next to him, Annie let out a soft gasp as the light came on in the front of the cabin.

"Bold," Wade murmured.

"Look who they are," she whispered back.

He peered through the darkness. One of the men was standing near the window, looking intently at the floor. After a second, he looked up, seemingly right at Wade.

Wade froze, even though he knew the light inside the cabin would turn the window into a mirror blocking out anything outside. The man stood there a moment before he turned away, but it was long enough for Wade to recognize him as one of the two fake A.F.O.S.I. agents who'd been keeping watch outside Annie's hospital room. The same men who'd chased them through the tunnel.

"They don't give up, do they?" she whispered. "Think they're looking for signs we were there?"

"Maybe. Or maybe they're looking for something else." Like whatever they'd kidnapped the Harlowes for in the first place. He and his family had assumed it was to find out what the three generals were hiding, but the bad guys already knew about the existence of General Ross's journal. They'd gone to a lot of trouble trying to steal it from Lydia Ross just a few weeks earlier, nearly killing Wade's sister in the process.

So what were these guys looking for? Keys to the code that had kept the journal unreadable so far, despite Shannon's best efforts to crack the cipher?

He glanced at Annie, who was watching the

movement of the two men inside through narrowed, thoughtful eyes. She looked different, he realized. Stronger and less nervous than she'd been even a few hours ago as they drove up the mountain toward the cabin.

What had happened when he'd left her alone inside her father's study? Had she remembered something else?

"They look like they're planning to stay awhile," Annie whispered.

She was right. They did. The light went off in the front room and came on again in one of the smaller rooms—General Harlowe's study, he realized. "You didn't leave any traces behind, did you?"

"I don't think so."

Shifting his position a little, Wade looked down the narrow drive and spotted a dark sedan in the driveway. It was parked several yards away from the house, which confused him for a moment until he realized the hard-packed dirt and gravel of the driveway wouldn't produce tire tracks the way the softer dirt closer to the house would.

These guys didn't want anyone to know they'd been here, either.

"Are they both in that room?" he whispered.

"I see two shadows."

He wondered if they'd left a third person to guard the car. "Wait here." He edge his way closer to the sedan, keeping the trees between him and the cabin's line of sight.

Of course, Annie didn't stay put. "Where are we going?"

He shot her a look of frustration. "Not much for waiting here?"

"You're not going to do what I think you're going to do, are you?"

"If you mean search their car? Yeah. That's what I'm going to do."

"Are you crazy?" Even though she was whispering, her voice rose an octave. "They'll see the dome light—"

"They can't see the car from where they are. Worry more about whether or not the car is locked." He slipped through the woods quietly, his attention fixed to the cabin even as he kept the car in his peripheral vision. The light in the front room remained off, but a soft glow through the windows showed that the other light was still on.

"You wait here and watch the cabin," he said.

"I can't see the cabin well from here. Plus, I'd have to shout for you to hear my warning." She lifted her chin. "I'll go with you. I'll play lookout."

He frowned, not wanting her to take such a desperate risk. But she was right. She'd make a much better lookout if she was closer to him, with a better view of the cabin. There was no easy way to do what he wanted to do.

He either had to let her take the risk, or call it off altogether.

He almost called it off. The idea of putting Annie at graver risk went against everything his Marine Corps training had drummed into him. Marines didn't risk the lives of civilians if there was any way to avoid it. And he had a way to avoid it. He could abort the mission.

But he might never have a better chance to get a close-up look at just what the S.S.U. mercenaries were up to. If there was anything in their car that Cooper Security could use to unravel whatever plot those guys were cooking up, he had to take the chance.

He might even come across a vital clue to the whereabouts of Annie's parents. Could he really walk away from that opportunity?

He couldn't. Not for Annie's sake. Nor for the sake of all his family had risked over the past few months to find out what this ruthless band of mercenaries was really up to.

"Okay," he said quietly, clasping her hand in his. "You stay as close to the tree line as you can. If you see any movement in the house, tell me and then get the hell out of sight. Understood?"

She nodded, gazing up at him with scared eyes. But her chin lifted and her shoulders squared. "Let's go."

The first obstacle was the door lock. There was

a possibility that the two men had locked the car behind them when they went inside, but Wade was gambling that they'd value a fast getaway more than vehicle security given their stealthy mission and the cabin's secluded location.

He was right. And, to his relief, the dome light Annie had worried about didn't engage when he opened the driver's door. They'd chosen to go dark. Cops often disabled their dome lights so that they could easily open the door without the dome light revealing their position.

So did the bad guys.

Annie crouched next to the car, her worried gaze pinned to the front of the cabin. "Just hurry!"

He took a risk and turned on the pen light, flicking the beam around the car's interior. The front seats were empty, almost pristine. There was a whiff of military precision to just how buttoned up the vehicle was, a reminder that for all their corruption, most of the S.S.U. operatives had been trained by professionals. It was a mistake to assume that evil intentions equaled sloppy procedures.

He closed the front car door as quietly as he could and tried the back door. The back was nearly as spotless as the front, save for a manila file folder lying on the floorboard behind the driver's seat.

Wade flipped the folder open and found a photo of Annie Harlowe staring back at him. It was her professional headshot, apparently commissioned by the D.C.-area newspaper she worked for. It was the same shot Jesse had supplied to all the Cooper Security operatives he'd assigned to the Harlowe case when they'd first been reported missing.

He flipped the photo to get to the next page. It was a one-sheeter on Annie Harlowe, listing her place of residence, her personal connections, her favorite haunts back in D.C. and elsewhere. It wasn't exactly like the dossier Jesse had compiled for them when they first started looking into the Harlowes' disappearance, but it was much the same.

After all, the S.S.U.'s current goal was similar to Cooper Security's previous one: find Annie Harlowe.

He flipped past the dossier, half hoping he'd find something similar on the other Harlowes. It might mean they'd managed to escape as well. But the next photo in the stack wasn't either of the elder Harlowes, which might mean a couple of different things. Either the S.S.U. still had custody of the Harlowes or they knew the Harlowes were no longer able to pose any sort of risk to them. Either way, it wasn't good news.

Nor was the photo now staring up at him from the folder. A pair of bright blue eyes stared out of a pretty oval face. Honey-brown hair framed her face in loose waves. Her pink lips were curved in an enigmatic smile.

Wade muttered a low curse.

"What?" Annie asked in a worried whisper.

Wade picked up the photo and showed it to her. Her eyes widened.

"That's Rita Marsh," she whispered. Her brow furrowed as the implications hit her. "Oh, no."

Wade looked at the sheet of paper that lay beneath the photo. It was a dossier on General Baxter Marsh's elder daughter, similar to the one the S.S.U. had gathered on Annie Harlowe. Where she worked, where she lived, who she socialized with. And at the bottom, written in bold, black pen strokes, the words *Millwood Presbyterian Church. 10/20, 2 p.m.* stood out like a neon warning sign.

"The light in the front room just came on!" Annie grabbed his arm.

Wade slid everything back into the folder and replaced it where it had earlier lain. He closed the back door quietly and grabbed Annie's hand.

They ran straight for the woods, not looking back until they'd reached the safety of the four entangled pines. Together they crouched, trying to stay quiet as they caught their breaths and waited anxiously for any sign that the men inside the cabin were about to leave.

"The light's off again," Annie whispered, her body trembling next to his. He wrapped his arm around her shoulder and pulled her closer, feeling a rush of sheer male pleasure as she leaned against him, turning her cheek toward him so that it brushed against his face.

Adrenaline could be a powerful aphrodisiac, and Wade found himself fighting hard against the urge to kiss her again. But Marine Corps training was harsh and relentless for a good reason, and the discipline and control his drill sergeants had pounded into his young skull full of mush paid off. He whipped the rush of desire under control.

"They're staying," he murmured as a light came on somewhere in the back of the cabin again. "Any idea what they're looking for?"

She didn't answer right away, drawing his gaze to her face. It was pale in the shaft of faint moonlight angling down through a narrow break in the trees. Her caramel eyes looked mysterious and dark, sending a spark of unease fluttering through his gut.

She was hiding something, he realized.

But what?

"I don't think we should stick around any longer," she whispered.

He couldn't argue.

They circled through the woods, Wade letting Annie lead the way, as she seemed nearly as surefooted and confident moving through these woods as he used to be navigating the woods of Gossamer Ridge. They reached the car, hidden behind a tall canopy of kudzu vines that had formed between a pair of broken tree trunks. They were lucky, Wade knew, that it was September and the vines were still lush and green. Within a couple of months, the vines would wither and the leaves would thin out and die off until spring brought new growth again.

They were far enough from the cabin that it was unlikely the two men wandering around inside could hear the Ram's engine. But Wade still drove quickly down the mountain road, determined to put as much distance between them and the S.S.U. agents as possible.

His heart still pounded wildly by the time they reached the motel. He parked a few doors down from their room and they walked the rest of the way, moving at a fast clip. Only after they were inside did either of them make a sound, and it was Annie, who burst into helpless laughter.

Wade watched her with surprise, not only because her mirth seemed out of tune with the frantic tension of the last half hour but also because he'd never heard her laugh that way before. It was full-throated and infectious, drawing a smile to his own lips.

She stared back at him and just laughed harder. He found laughter bubbling up in his own throat and gave in, aware that laughter was a much safer tension reliever than what he'd contemplated earlier in the woods.

They quieted down after a moment, and Annie

collapsed on the bed, faceup, staring at the ceiling. "That was just about the scariest thing I've ever done on purpose," she said.

"I wish I could say the same." He dropped onto the opposite bed. "How are you feeling? How's your head?"

She propped herself on her elbows and looked at him. "Fine, actually," she answered with a half smile. "How's your knee?"

With a blink of surprise, he realized it hadn't bothered him at all while they were up on the mountain, though he felt a little twinge of pain now from so much sustained use. But it wasn't a bad pain, he had to admit. A little muscle ache but nothing that would give him any real trouble.

"Not bad," he admitted.

Her smile lingered. "I have a theory."

He wasn't sure he liked the knowing look in her eyes, but he took the bait anyway. "What's that?"

"When you're not thinking about your knee, it doesn't bother you nearly as much as when you do."

He narrowed his eyes. "You're saying it's psychosomatic?"

"Well, no. Not the injury. But you're so focused on what you've lost that you've been ignoring what you still have."

He wanted to argue with her, but if he was absolutely honest with himself, he couldn't. She was right, at least about tonight. With a ticking clock and the constant pressure of trying to evade detection, he hadn't had a moment to think about his bad knee. He'd just pressed on, past the weakness and whatever twinges of pain he might have felt, just as he'd always done with minor aches and pains during his time in the Marines. No man's body was flawless, none free of twinges and the strains of hard work. Many a night he'd had to ice his shoulder or massage his calves after a twenty-mile training run carrying a hundred-pound pack on his shoulders.

*But a sore muscle isn't the same thing as having your knee blown off.*

"Don't overthink it, Wade."

He leaned toward her, irritated that she seemed to find him so easy to read. It made him feel naked. "You remembered something tonight," he threw back at her, preferring to be on offense rather than defense.

Her eyes widened slightly before she schooled her features to a calm neutrality. "A thing or two," she admitted.

But he could tell she was holding something back.

"It happened when you were in the study," he prodded her.

"Shouldn't you call your company and tell someone about the photo of Rita?" she asked.

He pulled out his phone, typed in a text message and sent it to his cousin Luke's phone. "There, done. Now, stop changing the subject."

She sat up and faced him, her eyes ablaze. "You want to kiss me."

He arched one eyebrow at her bold statement. "You must really want to change the subject."

She just smiled and stood up, walking slowly across the room toward him. "I do," she admitted, "but that doesn't mean I don't want to kiss you, too." She laid her palms on either side of his face. "Just to get it out of the way, I'll stipulate that doing this is probably all sorts of stupid, and I have no doubt that most of what we're both feeling right now is adrenaline fueled." She bent closer. "But I've been wanting to do this ever since we ran away from the cabin."

He couldn't have resisted her if he wanted to, especially when she lowered her mouth to his. She kissed him fiercely, soulfully, her hands tightening on his cheeks to hold him in place. Unwilling to relinquish total control, he wrapped his arms around her waist and pulled her down to the bed with him, pressing her deep into the mattress beneath him.

She wrapped her legs around his hips, tugging hard at the hem of his T-shirt. He wriggled against her, trying to aid her in her efforts, but the sound of his phone buzzing stilled them both.

"I have to get it," he groaned.

She breathed hard against his neck. "I know."

He rolled away from her, pulling his phone from his back pocket. There was a return text from Luke. What he read there made his stomach drop. "Oh, no."

Annie sat up next to him, looking over his shoulder at the text. "Oh my God," she whispered. "Is that the neighbor who agreed to watch your cat?"

Wade nodded, staring with sick horror at the phone display.

*George Foley found dead on your front porch this p.m. Murdered. Watch your back.*

## Chapter Eleven

"What about the cat?" Annie asked as she watched Wade pack their supplies. Her whole body still felt numb from the shock of Luke Cooper's last text message. She'd met George Foley briefly outside Wade's cabin, introduced to him as a cousin from Birmingham as Wade arranged for his neighbor to keep an eye on Ernie and make sure he was fed and spent the nights indoors.

"I don't know." He picked up the phone for the third time in the last five minutes, this time dialing a number. Annie got up and started packing where he'd left off, earning a small, grateful smile as he paced away from the bed while he waited for his cousin to pick up.

A moment later, he said, "Luke, it's me. Tell me what you know."

While Wade listened, anger and regret darkening his expression, Annie finished packing quickly, although from what she could glean from Wade's side of the conversation, Luke seemed to be urging him not to make any quick decisions.

"I know it's dangerous, but it's dangerous here, too." He told Luke about their visit to the cabin. Luke didn't seem to take the news well; Annie could hear his raised voice from where she stood.

"It's done, and it got us the information about Rita Marsh. Have you told Jesse yet?" After a brief pause, he said, "Well, do so as soon as you can. He needs to know."

Annie finished putting the last of their clothes and supplies in the bag and zipped it shut. Sitting on the edge of the bed, she watched Wade as the speed and power of his pacing increased. He was starting to limp a little now, though he clearly wasn't thinking about anything but the trouble at hand, a reminder that while he was in better condition that he thought, he wasn't 100 percent and might never be again.

But he was willing to put everything he had left on the line for her. She saw it in the fierce determination gleaming in his dark eyes and the power and intensity of his gaze when he looked at her. "I'll keep her safe," he said into the phone, but she knew it was a message to her, too.

She had to tell him about the code. It might end up being useless information, especially if they couldn't find the other generals' codes, but he'd earned the truth from her. And given the clear threat the S.S.U. posed to Rita Marsh—and the rest of her family, no doubt—it was the least she owed her father's old friend as well.

Wade said goodbye to his cousin and hung up the phone. "Ernie's fine. Shannon has taken him in for the time being."

"Do they know what happened to your neighbor?"

"Double-tapped in the back of the head. Luke said my house has been tossed as well."

"So they know I'm with you."

"Apparently." He sat beside her on the bed, close enough to touch. She didn't let herself give in to the temptation.

"Luke wants us to stay put?"

"He wants us to get out of here and go somewhere else. He suggested Canada," Wade added with a wry grin. "I don't think that's a good idea."

"What do you want to do?"

He sighed. "I want to go back home. My family is there. Safety in numbers and all that."

"It's dangerous to go back there."

"I'm afraid it's dangerous to go anywhere." Wade leaned forward, putting his head in his hands. "I'm sorry. Things seem to be getting worse the longer you stick with me."

"They'd get worse anywhere," she said quietly, echoing his earlier words. "I'm glad I'm with you."

He shot her a wry look. "You just want me for my body."

She laughed, as he'd clearly intended. "Well, sure. But I also trust you to have my back. You've already gone far beyond the call of duty."

"I'm going to tell you something," he said, a look of decision crossing his face. "It's something only a very few people know and you can't share it with anyone else."

*The code*, she thought. *He knows something about the code.*

"Last month, my sister Shannon worked a job for Lydia Ross, archiving her late husband's papers and collections. While she was there, she found something strange."

"A coded journal," Annie murmured, now certain she was right.

His gaze snapped up to meet hers. "You know about it?"

She nodded slowly. "I didn't remember before tonight, though."

"What do you know about it?" he asked warily.

"It's written in multilayered code that can be broken only if you have all three code keys," she said, watching his face carefully. He seemed surprised, though she didn't know whether it was what she was saying or the fact that she was saying it at all that confounded him the most.

"How do you know this?"

"My father told me about it, shortly before we were abducted."

Wade sat back, thrusting his fingers through his dark hair. "We think your father must have told the S.S.U. about the journal at some point of your captivity, because shortly after your abduction, a group of their agents went to a whole lot of trouble to get that journal away from Lydia Ross."

"My father wouldn't tell anyone about the journal," she protested.

"Not even to preserve your life? Or your mother's?"

She quelled the urge to insist he wouldn't, because in truth, while her father loved his country, there was nothing he loved more than his family. Knowing that all three layers of code would have to be broken before the journal would be any good to anyone, might he have revealed its existence in order to keep the S.S.U. thugs from harming his family?

It was a strong possibility, she had to admit. For all she knew, she herself had revealed the truth. There was a lot about her time in captivity she still couldn't remember.

What if the information about the journal had come from her?

She looked up at Wade with alarm. "Did they find it?"

"No," he admitted after a brief pause. "The journal is safe."

Relief raced through her. "Good."

"Do you know what's in it?" he asked.

Her father's voice rang in her mind. *Protect the code.*

But Wade Cooper wasn't with the S.S.U. He'd put his life on the line for her, lost a friend and neighbor for her. If he hadn't earned her trust by now, there was no one on earth who could.

"It's an outline of a far-reaching conspiracy my father and Generals Ross and Marsh uncovered during their mission in Kaziristan," she answered slowly, watching his face for his reaction.

He didn't look surprised this time. So he'd already had an idea about what the journal had contained.

But how had he learned about it?

"You already know this," she said.

He shook his head. "Suspected it," he admitted. "But we weren't sure what the journal contained because we haven't been able to break the code."

"You have to have all three code keys to break it," she repeated.

"Each general kept one of the keys?"

"Yes. All three had to have input before the contents made sense." Her gut twisted as she realized something that should have occurred to her before. "And with General Ross dead—"

"We don't have that part of the code, regardless," he finished for her. "But we're working an angle on that end that we're hoping will solve the problem."

"What kind of angle?"

He looked at her through slightly narrowed eyes, as if assessing how much he should share. "I don't know the details," he admitted. "I just know that the tech department is working hard at trying to bust the code."

"I doubt it can be broken without all three parts," she said bleakly. "Did General Ross know, before his death, that other people were looking for his journal?"

"I don't think so."

"Who would he have told his secrets to, if he were inclined to share?"

"At a guess, his son Ford."

"His son is dead," Annie said bleakly. "Killed in Kaziristan two years ago. So if General Ross told Ford his secrets—"

"We're trying to find out if he could have told someone else. We're in contact with his widow and also Ford's best friend."

"Maybe General Ross gave the information to someone without their realizing it. Maybe he told my father where to find the information if something ever happened to him. Which means he almost certainly told General Marsh as well."

"General Marsh won't take any of our calls.

He's even ignoring calls from his younger daughter these days."

"He has to know he's on someone's hit list after all this."

"I think he's probably more worried about his daughters," Wade said. "With good reason, considering what we found in that car tonight."

Annie rubbed her gritty eyes. "Do you think General Marsh told one of his daughters the key for his layer of code?"

Wade looked at her suddenly, realization gleaming in his dark eyes. "Your father gave you the key, didn't he?"

She stared at him, not sure how to answer. *Protect the code,* her father had told her. The best way to protect it was to let everyone think it no longer existed in any recoverable way.

But hadn't Wade earned her trust?

He had. But some things were more important than trust.

"No," she lied. "He didn't."

Wade looked briefly troubled by her statement, but soon his expression cleared. "You're probably safer that way."

Now she felt terrible for lying, even if it was to do what her father had asked her to do. "We'll be less likely to ever be able to break the code and protect what my father and the other generals knew."

"That's not my priority at the moment." He

looked at the bag Annie had finished packing. "I don't think we can stick around here any longer. You ready to go?"

She found her gaze wandering around the motel room, taking in the cramped, uninspired decor, and realized she'd felt safer here than she'd felt in a long time.

Because Wade had been with her.

"Where are we going, exactly?"

He picked up the bag. "The most secure place in Chickasaw County is the Cooper Security office building. Double layers of security, plus a whole building full of people who know how to fight like soldiers."

"So, what? We bunk down on desks or something?"

Wade just grinned at her. "Or something."

The trip back to Chickasaw County took three and a half harrowing hours, most of which Annie had spent certain that every passing car was full of S.S.U. agents determined to stop them. About halfway there, Wade pulled the Ram pickup into the parking lot of a twenty-four-hour truck stop near the I-59 on ramp and parked, shutting down the engine. Pulling his cell phone out of his pocket—the third time he'd done so during the long drive—he pecked a few times on the small keypad and hit Send.

"What now?" Annie asked warily.

"We go inside and have an early breakfast." He opened the driver's side door and climbed out of the cab, making a little grumbling noise as his bad knee took his weight.

He limped a little as he led her inside the truck stop diner, but the impairment would have been barely noticeable had she not been looking for it. She smiled behind his back as they took a seat at the counter, a few seats down from a small cluster of truckers who were drinking coffee and sharing road stories with a smiling middle-aged waitress.

A second waitress, a redhead in her early thirties, took their order with a stifled yawn. Wade ordered eggs, bacon and a biscuit, but Annie didn't think her nervous stomach could handle much more than a glass of milk and a piece of toast. The waitress nearly rolled her eyes at the order but headed to the back to hand it off.

"Should we be out in the open like this?" Annie asked.

Wade just smiled. "We're going to be on the road a long time. Can't starve ourselves or we won't make it far." Beneath the counter, he caught her hand and gave it a squeeze.

She looked up at him and saw his gaze slant upward for a second. He squeezed her hand again.

Slowly, she let her eyes drift upward and spotted a security camera. She blinked, lowering her gaze while her eyes were shut, and hoped it had looked natural.

"Where next?" she asked aloud, striving to keep her voice normal. She didn't know if the security camera had audio recording capabilities, but just in case...

"Jesse said he has a friend in Minnesota who could get us across the border without anyone asking questions," Wade said. "I'm afraid we're in for a lot more driving."

The waitress brought their plates and handed them their receipt. Wade pulled his wallet out and paid the bill, then unhurriedly ate his breakfast.

Annie nibbled her toast and tried not to freak out completely. Clearly Wade had a plan of some sort. She had to trust he knew what he was doing.

But when they went out to the truck to find it tightly flanked on both sides by two dark panel vans, she felt panic rise in her throat.

"Steady," Wade said in a low voice, threading his fingers through hers.

As they reached the truck, the front doors of the van on the left opened, and two men got out, one tall and blond, the other shorter and dark-haired. They headed up the walk to the truck stop.

The second they were inside, the panel door of the van on the left slid open, making Annie's heart skip a beat. Two people emerged, a dark-haired woman about Annie's size and a dark-haired man who looked enough like Wade to be his brother, though it wasn't Jesse Cooper, whom she'd met briefly in the car that helped her escape the hospital.

Wade handed over the truck keys to the man, who unlocked the pickup and climbed into the driver's side of the cab. The dark-haired woman stopped, pointed to Annie's denim jacket and held out her hands. Annie took off the jacket and handed it to her. The woman put it on and walked around the truck, climbing into the passenger side.

"In the van," Wade murmured, waving his hand toward the open door.

Annie looked into the van and found Isabel Cooper looking back at her, an encouraging smile on her face. She held out her hand to Annie.

With a deep breath, she took it and let Wade's sister help her inside.

Wade climbed up behind her and they settled into one of the two bench seats in the enclosed body of the van while Isabel closed the door.

"The vans blocked the security camera's view of the truck," Wade explained. Outside the van, the truck's engine roared to life, then faded away as the truck apparently left the lot. A moment later, the other van started and drove away as well, heading in the opposite direction.

"Who were those people?" Annie asked.

"The two guys who went into the diner are Terry

Allen and Dennis McCready. Terry and Mac. The guy in the van is Mason Hunter, one of our field agents. The man and woman are my cousin Troy Cooper and Delilah Hammond, another of our field agents," Isabel answered, settling on the bench seat in front of them. She buckled herself in. "Troy looks a lot like Wade, obviously. And Delilah is the closest to you in size and coloring we could find on short notice."

"Didn't we just send them out as decoys for the S.S.U. to follow?" Annie asked with alarm. "What if they try to ambush them?"

"Delilah spent several years in FBI special ops, and Troy was a Navy SEAL for over a decade before retiring this past spring and joining Cooper Security to help us go after the S.S.U.," Wade answered. "They know the risks and they know what they're doing."

Annie still didn't like it. "What now?"

"Mac and Terry eat breakfast." Wade checked his watch. "We have about fifteen minutes to decompress."

"I don't think I'll be doing much of that," Annie muttered, her hand over her still-racing heart.

"It's the best way we could figure to get you to the Cooper Security office without anyone knowing it," Isabel said. "There are still people watching."

"How did you get away unseen?" Annie asked. "Isn't there someone following you, too?"

"Scanlon and I went to Huntsville last night to see a concert. Our car's still parked in the hotel parking lot, and Scanlon's in the room, with the do-not-disturb sign on the door." She shot Annie a wry grin. "Sadly, I'm not there with him, but my phone is, so if anyone's figured out a way to track me by my cell signal, they should think I'm in there, too. As soon as we get underway, Mac will drop Terry and me off where I left my getaway car and we'll be heading back there to reunite me with my phone and my husband in time to check out."

"This is all very cloak and dagger," Annie said.

"It's kind of what we do." Wade caught her hand and gave it a reassuring squeeze. When he started to let go, she held on, twining her fingers through his. He gave her a long, smoldering look that did wonders to drive off the chill that had settled deep in her bones during the harrowing drive from Georgia.

The two men who'd left the van returned, not even acknowledging the rest of them as they climbed into their seats and the driver started the engine. Only when they were a mile down the road from the truck stop did the blond man in the passenger seat turn to look at them. "Terry Allen," he introduced himself to Annie. "This is Dennis McCready. Goes by Mac."

"I've caught them up on what we're doing," Isabel said.

"There's something else you need to know," Terry said, his gaze encompassing all three of them. Annie felt Wade grow tense beside her.

"What?" Isabel asked.

Terry looked straight at Annie. "Fort Payne authorities have found your mother."

## Chapter Twelve

Annie's grip on Wade's hand tightened in a painful vise. He looked away from Terry's grim face to Annie's and saw her fear playing out across her face like a movie.

"Is she dead?" she asked, her voice cracking.

"She's alive," Terry said quickly. "That's all Jesse's text said."

Annie turned to look at Wade. "I have to go to her."

"It could be a trap," Isabel warned.

"That's what Jesse thinks, too." Mac spoke for the first time, his low, gravelly voice forceful, despite its quiet tone. He met Wade's gaze in the rearview mirror, his eyes speaking volumes.

"She needs me," Annie insisted. She let go of Wade's hand, edging away from him as if setting up defenses against all of them.

"I know she does," Isabel soothed, "and as soon as we can prove it's not a trap, we'll get you to her."

"I need to go to her now!" Annie's voice rose.

She made a visible effort to control her spiraling emotions, her chin trembling. "If she knows anything about what happened to her, I may be the only person she'd tell."

"Let's just get to Cooper Security and see what's what," Wade suggested. He reached out to take her hand again, but she pulled it away. He let his hand drop back to his lap.

"Fine," Annie said in a low, tight voice. "But the decision is mine."

He looked at Isabel. She gazed back at him with a mixture of curiosity and understanding.

"Okay," he said, even though the thought of letting Annie put her life in any more danger made his stomach hurt. "The decision is yours."

The drive from the truck stop to Cooper Security took another hour, longer than it would have if Mac hadn't doubled back a few times and taken a circuitous route to make sure they hadn't been followed. They also had to drop off Terry and Isabel at the wasting shell of Old Saddlecreek Church, an abandoned church nestled in the shadow of Gossamer Mountain. It hadn't seen a congregation in years, but the weathered clapboard building still stood, sagging a bit and marred in places by local teenage vandals.

As soon as Terry and Isabel were out of the van, Mac drove on, not waiting to make sure they got safely to the waiting car. They had a job to do, and so did he. If Isabel and Terry needed backup, they'd put out a distress signal and backup would be on the way.

"Did the call about my mother come in while you were at the truck stop?" Annie asked. She still sat stiff and distant, even though she was buckled into the bench seat only a few inches away from Wade.

"Jesse sent a text. I couldn't make a big deal of looking at the text, in case anyone was watching." Mac glanced at them in the rearview mirror. "We ate as fast as we could to get back here to tell you."

"And she's definitely alive?"

"Yes. Jesse said to be sure to tell you that."

She took a long, shaky breath, and Wade felt a strong urge to put his arm around her and pull her close. But she showed no signs of softening her rigid posture, so he kept his hands to himself.

They reached Cooper Security just as sunrise was beginning to peek through the trees to the east. Mac pulled the van into the covered parking garage at the far end of the building and found a space near the elevators.

"Home sweet home," he murmured, getting out of the van.

Wade turned to look at Annie and found her gazing back at him. "Home?"

He nodded. "Come on. Let me show you a part of Cooper Security that most folks don't know anything about."

THE WHOLE WEST END OF Cooper Security, all three stories of it, seemed to comprise a dormitory, Annie discovered as she followed Wade down a wide corridor just off the elevator alcove.

"Technically, there are enough rooms to accommodate every Cooper Security agent and his or her immediate family in the case of an emergency," Wade explained as he stopped at one of the doors, numbered 321. "This is my designated room." He pulled his keys from his pocket and unlocked the door, revealing a small, spare bedroom inside.

There was a smaller room, barely larger than a closet, that contained a toilet and a sink but no tub or shower. "There's a communal shower for men at the north end of the hall on this floor. The south end has the women's shower. Some cases, we're working a lot of hours and it's just easier to grab a few hours of sleep and a quick shower than to go home and come back."

"And in the case of a terrorist attack—"

"We can bring our families and loved ones here where they'll be safer."

"So you can do your work without having to worry about them."

He smiled at her. "That, too."

She looked at the lone bed, a comfortable-looking full-sized bed that could easily accommodate one but might be a close fit for two, and drove the obvious question from her mind. It didn't matter anymore. Not until she saw her mother. "I need to see Jesse."

Wade nodded and crossed to a phone on the bedside table. He picked up the receiver and punched in a number. "We're here," he said a moment later. "She wants answers."

He hung up. "Jesse's on his way."

While she stood at the end of the bed, trying not to let the trembling in her knees take over the rest of her body, Wade put their supply bag on the bed and unzipped it. "I'll leave your stuff inside," he said, starting to remove his own extra clothes and their supplies from the bag.

Before he had finished, there was a sharp rap on the door that made Annie's nerves rattle.

Wade put his hand out to stay her automatic move to the door and crossed in front of her, checking through the peephole in the door. She hadn't even noticed it there before, she realized, wondering just how much danger these people expected that they'd put a peephole in an internal dormitory door.

Wade's posture relaxed and he opened the door, admitting the dark-haired man who'd driven the getaway car that had aided their earlier escape from the hospital—his older brother, Jesse, the CEO of Cooper Security.

Jesse gave Wade a quick, fierce hug and then turned quickly to Annie. "I guess you have questions."

"I want to see my mother."

"I'm sure you do, but I need to give you all the facts before you do anything."

"You're stalling me."

"Annie, just listen—" Wade put his hand on her shoulder.

She shrugged it off. "Don't try to handle me."

"Your mother is in good condition, but she doesn't remember anything about what happened," Jesse said. "The FBI got to her before we did. Luckily, our cousin Will was one of the agents assigned to talk to her, and the FBI has given him permission to share the basics of their conversation with your mother with us."

Annie swallowed her impatience, beginning to understand that throwing a fit wouldn't make Jesse Cooper reveal the information she wanted any faster. She took a deep breath and asked the most important question. "What are her injuries?"

"She doesn't have a concussion or any major injuries. She's dehydrated, and like you, she has some ligature marks on her wrists and ankles, but no signs of torture or other physical mistreatment."

"So why doesn't she remember?"

"The doctors think she may have been kept sedated the whole time she was in captivity," Jesse answered.

"Put on ice," Wade murmured.

Annie whipped her gaze around to look at him. "Put on ice?"

"You were the more obvious leverage against your father," he said. "A man's desire to protect his child is even stronger than his desire to protect his wife. You're also younger, which meant you could probably take more abuse than your mother could, for a longer amount of time."

"Plus, you're a journalist who covered the Barton Reid story," Jesse added. "It's more likely you'd know more than your mother did about what your father was hiding."

"Mother made a point of maintaining ignorance of my father's secrets," she admitted. "She was his safe haven where he could leave that all behind."

"The doctor wants to keep her overnight tonight to make sure she doesn't get any more dehydrated," Jesse said. "Meanwhile the FBI has her under guard and plans to take her into protective custody as soon as she's cleared to leave the hospital."

"How did she get away?" Annie asked. "Does she remember?"

"She doesn't know," Jesse told her. "She told Will that she woke up in a field at the side of the road just outside Fort Payne. She managed to flag down a passing car. The occupants called paramedics and the police. But she has no idea how she got to the field."

Which meant she hadn't escaped, Annie realized. She'd been let go, left at the side of the road to be found.

She sat heavily on the end of Wade's bed, realizing suddenly why nobody at Cooper Security wanted her to rush off to her mother's side.

"It's a trap," she said.

"That's what we think," Jesse said quietly.

Annie looked from him to Wade. "Does my mother know I'm safe?"

"Will told her you had escaped and were in protective custody," Jesse answered. "It seemed to calm her quite a bit, though she is obviously still distressed about your father still being missing."

Her mother wasn't alone in that concern. Annie wasn't sure how to interpret her mother's unexpected release. Did it make her father's continued existence more vital than ever? Or was he now considered expendable?

Wade touched her shoulder once more. This time she let his hand remain in place, feeling ashamed of her earlier prickliness. Wade was not her enemy. On the contrary, he was about the only person she trusted at the moment to have her best interests in mind.

Including herself.

Left to her own instincts, she'd have hurried right to her mother's bedside, the risk to her own life be damned. But looking at the situation more rationally and less emotionally, she could see that her mother's unexpected release, so close to where Annie herself had turned up only a few days earlier, almost certainly was a trap to lure her back into her captors' control.

"What do we do now?" she asked.

"I've rerouted Troy and Delilah," Jesse answered. "They'll head for the hospital in Fort Payne to see your mother. I have five other agents trailing them, looking for an ambush."

"I don't like them putting their lives in danger for me that way."

"They know what kind of work they signed on for," Wade said quietly. "We all do."

"So in the meantime, what do we do?"

Wade's grip on her shoulder tightened. "We wait."

"WHO'S LEFT IN THE BUILDING?" Wade paced in a tight circle near the end of the hallway, just a few feet from the women's shower room, within easy earshot. Clearly, Jesse thought, his younger brother didn't like the idea of letting Annie Harlowe out of his sight for even a few minutes. But she'd pleaded for a hot shower, and, short of showering with her, standing guard outside was the only way to appease Wade's need to keep her safe.

Jesse watched him pace, a hint of amusement mingling with the overriding weight of responsibility he felt for not only the hunted woman inside the shower room but also his brother. Jesse had been the one who'd convinced Wade to stop beating his head against the Marine Corps wall and join Cooper Security instead. He had begun to wonder if he'd made a mistake, but Wade's brief stint as Annie Harlowe's personal guardian had done wonders for his brother's demeanor.

"Three guards—Hotchkiss, Fordham and Fiorello," he answered Wade's question. "I plan to stick around for the night, too. Oh, and I think there may be somebody left in the accounting section, too. I noticed lights on down the hall." Quarterly reports were due by the end of the month, although the staff rarely stayed this late in the evening.

"Three guards, plus us? Is that it?" Wade asked. Jesse didn't miss his brother's look of displeasure.

Annie Harlowe emerged suddenly from the showers, her hair wrapped in a towel. She wore a T-shirt and a pair of soft yoga pants and looked stronger than she had before she went into the shower. "There are only three guards here?" she asked, looking alarmed.

"We wanted to keep a low profile." Jesse lowered his voice by habit, even though the three of them were the only people in the dormitory wing.

"So they don't realize I'm here?" Annie guessed.

"What if they figure out she's here and decide now is the perfect time to strike?" Wade countered, his jaw squared rebelliously. "We'd be outnumbered and then what?"

"We still have layers of security they'd have to get through. And an arsenal of weapons at our disposal."

"If we have time to get to them."

Jesse didn't miss the way his brother's gaze kept gravitating to Annie Harlowe's pale face. So Wade *did* have a personal stake in this case. Not the ideal situation—Jesse much preferred his agents to be levelheaded and logical rather than emotional about their jobs—but he couldn't begrudge his brother a little bit of happiness in life. If Annie Harlowe turned out to be the girl for Wade, he could do worse.

And he'd certainly have extra incentive to keep her safe. Since she might be Cooper Security's best chance of getting her father back alive—and getting access to his part of the code— it was in all their best interests to keep Annie Harlowe alive and kicking.

"I'm going to head back to my office for a while. I have some paperwork piling up. Call if you need anything."

"Wait." Wade grabbed his arm. "Have you talked to Luke?"

"Of course."

"Aren't you freaking out about Rita being a target? They had the date of her upcoming wedding written down, along with the church where it'll take place."

Jesse tried to hide his feelings. He knew he was probably unsuccessful, though his voice came out calm enough. "I heard. They're probably going to try to make a move on the Marsh family during the wedding. Unfortunately, none of us is invited."

"Evie will be there," Wade said.

She was an accountant, not a security agent. "I know she's had training, but—"

"I just meant, maybe you could talk her into taking you for her date."

"Oh." It was worth a try, he supposed. "Whether she will or won't, I think we should have a presence there. Out of sight."

Wade nodded. "Absolutely."

"It's on my to-do list," Jesse told his brother, hoping his anxiety didn't show. He knew his siblings still worried about how his breakup with Rita had affected him, even though it had happened years ago. But none of them could afford the distraction.

"Thank you for your help," Annie said.

"You're welcome." He clapped his brother's back and headed for the stairs at the end of the hall, bypassing the elevators. Since trading in his combat utility uniform for civilian clothes, he'd found it harder and harder to keep his fighting shape, even with an on-premises gym. So he made a point of eschewing the elevators and taking the stairs.

It wasn't quite the same as a trek up a snowy mountain in full gear, but it was better than nothing. Especially with a full load of adrenaline coursing through him, thanks to his worry about Rita and her family.

He reached the second floor offices and had started toward his big corner suite when he noticed lights still on in the accounting section. Curious, he reversed course and entered the communal office where the company's number crunchers carried on their work.

The office was empty save for a small, dark-haired woman sitting at a computer near the back. Her shoulder-length hair was twisted up at the back of her head, anchored there by a pencil, and her dark blue eyes were focused on the computer screen that lit her face pale blue.

So intent was her focus that Jesse made it within a few feet of her before her gaze snapped up and she gave a small start, pressing her hand to her chest. "God, Jesse, could you make a little noise next time?"

"Situational awareness is vital for all Cooper Security employees," he said softly, quoting the company employee manual.

She made a face he wouldn't let most employees get away with. But Evie Marsh wasn't most employees. She was the sister of the woman Jesse had once thought he wanted to spend the rest of his life loving.

And he just might need her help protecting her sister at her wedding.

"I'll put in extra time at the training session next week," she promised. "Actually, I'm glad you're still here. I need to show you something."

"What kind of something?"

Evie's brow furrowed as she met his curious gaze. "I hate to say it, but I'm beginning to suspect one of the employees is up to something fishy."

"How LONG DO YOU THINK it will take your friends to get to the hospital?"

At Annie's question, Wade stopped unpacking their things and turned to look at her. She sat in the middle of his bed, her legs tucked under her. She looked tired but beautiful, and Wade wondered if it would be safer for both of them if he called Jesse and asked him to provide another room for Annie for the night. "I don't know. It depends on how far north they got before they got the call to reverse course."

"My mother must be terrified. All alone, nobody there for her but armed guards." Annie shook her head. "She was so relieved when my dad finally retired from the Air Force that she nearly threw a party."

"She didn't like his being in the military?"

"No, I don't want to make it sound like that," Annie said quickly, shaking her head. "Mom was very proud of my dad and his service. She was proud of being an Air Force wife and keeping the home fires lit. She took it very seriously—doing her patriotic duty just as my dad was doing his. She always made sure I understood why my dad had to be away from home so much. She was a rock. But having him home all the time, not having to worry when he went out the door to his job—I know it was a huge relief."

"Retirement for her, too?"

"Exactly."

Wade pulled up the only chair in the room so he could sit near her. He reached out tentatively to touch her hand. "I think she still remembers how to be a patriot, don't you?"

Annie's expression softened and she curled her hand until it was palm up against his. "Yes. I just hoped she wouldn't have to go back into service again, especially not this way. Not knowing where my dad is or if he's even going to come back to us alive—" Tears sparkled in her eyes. She blinked them away, not letting them fall.

"They'll keep him alive, you know."

She looked at him through narrowed eyes. "No, I don't know."

"They wouldn't be looking for you if your father had given them the code, would they?"

She gave it a moment's thought, then shook her head. "No, probably not. It's not like the people who took us aren't already wanted by the authorities, right? So they're not coming after me because they're afraid I can testify against them."

"Right. They're after you because they've figured out that you're the best leverage they can use against your father, which means he's still got to be alive, right? Or they wouldn't need the leverage."

Her troubled expression didn't shift at all. "Or it could mean something else," she said quietly, sliding her eyes upward to meet his.

The pain and fear in her eyes made his gut clench. "Like what?"

"There's something I haven't told you about the night the men broke into our cabin and abducted us," she said in a low, strangled tone. "Something my father told me just before it happened."

"Besides telling you about the coded journal?"

"Yes." She let go of his hand and sat back a little, wrapping her arms around her waist as if she were suddenly cold. "I told you that he explained how he and the other two generals decided to write down their suspicions and keep it safe by triple-encrypting their words. But that he hadn't given me the code so I'd be able to fill in the blanks if something ever happened to him."

"Right." Wade's eyes narrowed. "So what haven't you told me?"

"I lied," she blurted out, looking utterly miserable. "He did give me the code. And I'll bet the S.S.U. knows I have it."

## Chapter Thirteen

The look on Wade's face made Annie's heart contract. "You lied?"

"I'm sorry," she said, meaning it. "I wanted to tell you but—"

"But your father told you not to tell anyone." He looked away. "And I'm a stranger to you."

She reached out blindly, grabbing his arm. "You're not a stranger."

"It's okay. I understand."

She tightened her grip on his arm, not sure why she was so desperate to make him understand. Wouldn't it be smarter, wiser to let this rift starting to form between them continue growing? The last thing she needed was to have her reckless feelings for Wade Cooper continue complicating her already overcomplicated life.

But letting him think she didn't trust him was more than she could bear. He'd earned her trust, and she'd been wrong to withhold it from him, no matter what her reason. "I should have told you."

"I guess your father told you not to tell anyone?"

"Right." She loosened her tight grip on him, turning her touch into a caress. He looked down at her hand, watching her fingers play lightly over his bicep. "But I'm telling you now."

There was a hint of a smile on his face when he lifted his gaze to meet hers. "Why's that?"

She touched his face. "Because you deserve my trust."

He caught her hand, gently removing it from his cheek. "I'm not sure that's really true."

"You've protected me this whole time. And I don't believe for a second it's just because you think I can help you out in some way."

"That's part of it."

"But not all of it." She edged closer, unfolding her legs until they dangled over the side of his bed. She faced him fully now, reaching across the narrow space between them to cradle his face with both hands. "You know that's not all of it."

He gazed back at her, the expression on his face a mixture of consternation and helpless desire. "You're so damned sexy when you're deadly serious. Anybody ever told you that?"

Not many people had ever told her she was sexy, period. She'd been wary about letting people get too close in her line of work. Too many people in the world in which she lived were out there working their own agenda, willing to lie to a person's face to get an edge on an opponent or steal a story out from under her.

Sex was a weapon, intimacy a trick, a relationship a carefully calibrated business arrangement where one side always got the better end of the deal. The only love she'd ever really believed in was the one between her parents.

But Wade Cooper wasn't playing any angles. She didn't know if he even had that sort of deceit in him.

"Nobody's ever told me that," she admitted, running the pad of her thumb lightly over his bottom lip. "Has anyone ever told you that you're sexy every second of the day?"

His eyes narrowed slightly. "No, definitely not."

"Well, that's a damned shame." She bent toward him, her gaze on his firm, well-shaped mouth.

He caught her arms in his hands, keeping her at a short distance. "This isn't a good idea."

"Why not?" she asked, resisting his attempt to keep her at arm's length.

He tightened his grip and gently nudged her back toward the bed. "Because I'm not who you think I am."

"SOMETHING FISHY?" Jesse grabbed an empty chair from the desk next to Evie's and sat beside her, noticing that despite the long day and her otherwise disheveled appearance, she still smelled clean, like the woods after a hard rain. The scent hit him hard, right between the eyes, making his head swim for a second.

Disturbed by the unexpected reaction, his first instinct was to pull away from her. But she was already talking to him, clearly oblivious to his discomfiture, forcing him to slide closer in order to follow what she was telling him.

"I've been working on processing the expense vouchers before the big quarterly report presentation, and I've come across something odd about Derek Fordham's reports."

"Odd how?"

"Well, let's start with his miles. He was gone from the office on business ten days last month and logged one hundred and forty-three billable miles. But I checked that against the logged mileage on his vehicle—you know the fleet manager checks every time an agent brings a car back in. There are only seventy-nine miles listed on those vehicles he used."

He looked up at her and felt another odd twinge of vertigo. Looking down to clear his brain, he said, "We allow people to bill hours on their personal vehicles."

"I know. But the agents still have to log in the mileage of their personal vehicles before they're allowed to expense those miles."

"And Fordham didn't?"

"No, he did," Evie said. "But his mileage was way, way out of whack for the last month." She pointed to a column on her spreadsheet. "This is how many miles were on his personal vehicle when the fleet manager checked it at the beginning of the month. He only claimed sixty-four work-related miles. But look at his month's mileage."

Jesse looked at the number she pointed out and gave a slight start. "Eight hundred and seventy-three miles in one month?"

"I checked but he wasn't on vacation, and in fact, he worked overtime last month, clocking in nearly sixty hours a week including working each Saturday." She picked up a sheet of paper lying on her desk. "This is his work dossier. He lives on Black-briar Road, which is only two miles from the office. That's four miles a day for twenty-five work days—one hundred miles. And he was off only six days, and only a day or two at a time. Unless he took one hell of a road trip on one of those days, how did so many miles get on his car?"

"A girlfriend?"

"Lives alone. No girlfriend, boyfriend or otherwise—I checked around." Evie paused for a moment, sliding a sidelong glance his way.

He narrowed his eyes, his gut tightening. Not with anger, as he might have expected, given that one of his office support employees had run her own unauthorized investigation into another employee, but with worry. "What do you mean, you checked around?"

Her gaze dropped to her hands. "I might have followed him on his lunch hour a couple of times. And asked about him." Her dark lashes lifted, her blue eyes slanting toward him again. "I might have hinted that I found him really cute and wanted to know if he was available."

Now he was angry. "Evie, have you lost your mind? You can't just go around doing investigations into other employees! You can't go around doing investigations at all—you're not an agent. You're an accountant!"

"I know, but it was strange, and y'all are all so wrapped up in this Harlowe case—" She sighed. "I didn't want to bother you about this if there wasn't anything to it. So I did a little preliminary groundwork, that's all."

"That's too much." He should fire her, he thought. Just terminate her now, give her a good job reference and let her go be a staff accountant at some boring firm where she wouldn't be tempted to play girl detective.

He never should have hired Rita Marsh's little sister in the first place.

"Oh, wait," she said, just before he opened his mouth to give her the sack. He bit back the words and looked at her expectantly, but she was looking at the computer screen again. He followed her gaze and saw she was opening her email program. There was a new message with the subject line, "Derek Fordham inquiry." The email address wasn't familiar.

"What have you done?" he murmured.

"Just a sec." She opened the email, which was a formal letter from a real estate agent. The email was addressed to her, providing a list of tenants at the Bellewood Towers in Dallas, Texas, during a period from January to November four years earlier.

The list included a brokerage firm, a couple of law firms, an ad agency and a name that made Jesse's breath catch in his throat.

MacLear Security, Inc. was the fifth name on the list.

"Oh, no," Evie murmured.

He looked at her. "What is this list?"

She met his gaze, her blue eyes troubled. "Daughtry Security provided the building security for the Bellewood Towers. Derek Fordham worked for Daughtry at the time MacLear had offices in the building."

Jesse's blood chilled in his veins. "And Fordham is one of the security guards who's keeping watch here tonight."

Wade laid his hands on his knees to keep from touching Annie again and met her confusion-filled gaze. "I'm not a hero. Not anymore. Not ever."

"Isn't that up to me to judge?" she asked.

"Look, all I've ever been is a grunt. Enlisted straight out of high school, marched in the mud for years, crawled on my belly in the cold and the heat, in rain and in desert sand, and did what I was told. Couldn't shoot a rifle worth a damn, except maybe to save my own skin and the life of the man in the foxhole next to me." He shook his head. "Jesse hired me because I'm his brother. Lord knows I don't have any marketable skills besides being pretty good cannon fodder."

"Stop it." She grabbed his hands. "If you don't want things to go any further with us, just say so. You don't have to cut yourself down that way."

He twined his fingers with hers, unable to stop himself. "I want to kiss you right now so much it hurts. But I'm smart enough to know when someone is way out of my league."

"Again, isn't that up to me to judge?" She gave him a pointed look. "I don't know what's going to happen in the next hour, so I'm not exactly in the position to make any long-term commitments anyway. Why don't we just accept this thing between us for what it is?"

He couldn't hold back a smile. "Which is what?"

A little crease of consternation formed between her eyebrows. "Why do we have to define it anyway?" She tugged him closer. "If you want to kiss me, just kiss me."

"Annie?"

"Here, I'll make it easy for you." She pushed to her feet and stepped between his knees, her hips pressing against his ribcage, making his heart rattle like a snare drum. She let go of his hands to slide her fingers through his hair, tilting his face up to hers. "I want to kiss you. That okay with you?"

He closed his eyes and nodded.

Time seemed to stop as he waited to feel her lips on his once again. The tension grew so exquisite, he could hardly take a breath.

She dropped her hands away from his hair and he heard the creak of bedsprings. He opened his eyes and found her sitting on the edge of his bed again, her eyes on the floor.

"Okay, now I'm confused," he murmured, his whole body tingling with frustration.

Annie twined her fingers together in her lap. "I'm not really very good at relationships."

Wade stifled a smile. "Who is?"

"No, I mean, I'm really bad. I'm sort of notorious for how disastrous my social life is. I once had a blind date with an escaped felon."

A laugh escaped his throat.

"I'm serious!" she insisted. "That's the last time I'll let a confidential informant set me up on a date."

Wade shook his head, still smiling. "You're beautiful and smart and funny—I can't believe you have trouble attracting men."

"Oh, I attract them. But they're all married or predators or way too nice to put up with me for very long." She pushed her hair away from her face. "I work crazy hours and I'm on assignments sometimes days and weeks at a time. My best friends are cutthroat journalists and seedy informants. My dad's an Air Force general, which seems to fascinate all the wrong people and repel all the otherwise right people."

"If it repels them, are they really the right people?"

She shook her head. "No."

"When we found you, I did some reading about your background, so I could help you better. And you know what struck me more than anything else in my research?"

"What?"

"Your parents have been married for thirty years, and your father has been rising in the Air Force almost all of that time, spending months and years away from your mother and you. And yet, in all that time, there wasn't even a whiff of trouble in their marriage. No battlefield affairs for your dad, no stateside flirtations for your mom. Everyone we talked to—everyone—seemed downright envious of them."

Annie smiled. "They're crazy about each other. Always have been."

"Don't you want that for yourself?"

"Of course I do." She looked up at him, her eyes shining with pain. "I've just stopped looking. Because I don't think it exists outside of a few very rare instances."

Wade wanted to argue with her, but how could he? His own experience supported her theory. Sure, his brother Rick had recently lucked into a relationship that seemed to make both him and his new wife happy. And all three of his sisters were madly in love—Megan and Izzy were newlyweds, and Shannon would probably be engaged, if not married, before Christmas. But Jesse's one great love was about to marry somebody else and Wade himself hadn't had a serious long-term relationship since high school.

"What are you thinking about?" Annie asked.

"How I'd like to argue with you about the odds of finding that someone special. But I guess I can't."

"Your sister Isabel and her husband seem happy."

He nodded. "They are. But they came really close to losing it all. And don't get me started on my parents."

Her eyebrow arched. "What about your parents? Divorced?"

"No. Just separated."

She frowned sympathetically. "For how long?"

"Twenty-two years."

"What?"

"Seventeen years into the marriage, my mom

decided motherhood and marriage wasn't really for her. At least, not in any conventional way. So she left us with Dad and went off to find herself or something."

"Without any warning?"

"Jesse said he had an inkling, but he was nearly sixteen when she left. The rest of us were younger. Shannon wasn't even in kindergarten yet."

"That's terrible."

"I think with some time and distance, most of us have come to see it was probably the best thing she could have done for us. She was miserable being a mom, and not terribly good at it. Letting us go allowed us to find better mother figures in our lives. It worked out."

"Still, it must have given you a really skewed idea about love and marriage." She tucked her knees up to her chest—a protective posture, Wade thought. If he could get his bum knee up to his chest, he might be sitting much the same way, as tough as this conversation was turning out to be. "That's what scares me, I guess. That it's so much easier to find bad examples of romance than good ones these days. It makes sense to just keep your distance from someone else, doesn't it?"

"What makes you think I do that?" he asked, his tone light.

She shot him a wry grin. "I see the panic in your

eyes. If you didn't have to protect me, you'd have run screaming out of here ten minutes ago."

He laughed. "Frankly, I'm kind of enjoying talking to someone who appears to be as rotten at this relationship stuff as I am. We could form our own bowling team or something."

She smiled back at him, but it faded quickly. "I tell myself I don't want to be tied down in a relationship. I'm independent and successful at my work, and I don't need a man to come home to—"

"But you don't really believe it."

She met his gaze. "When I woke up and discovered my parents were missing, my first thought was how utterly alone I was without them. Even though we don't even live in the same state, I always knew I could call my mom or my dad to talk if I had something on my mind. And suddenly, I had something terrible happen to me and there was no one to talk to." She brushed tears from her eyes. "But then, suddenly, you were there. All the time, every time I opened my eyes or turned around."

"Like a bad penny."

"Like a lifeline." She unfolded her legs, dropped her feet to the floor and leaned forward, touching his face. "And I want you. I want you with me. I want you to hold me, to let me hold you." She dropped her hand to his bad knee. "I want to take away your pain and help you get better. I want to know what it feels like to wake up in your arms in the morning."

She spoke the words flatly, straightforwardly, without a hint of provocation. But their seductive power nearly ripped the breath from his lungs. Not just because she was confessing her desire for him but because her words so perfectly summed up how he was feeling as well.

"You feel it, too, don't you?" she asked, rising to stand over him again.

He stood, cradling her face between his hands. "Yes."

"Does it scare you as much as it scares me?"

He bent his head, resting his forehead against hers. "Yes."

"What are we going to do?"

"Stop thinking about it so much," he answered, bending to kiss her.

She rose to her toes, wrapping her arms around his neck and pulling him closer, her body aligning with his so exquisitely he had the crazy sensation that she'd been created specifically for him, and he for her. Her mouth was perfect, soft where it should be soft and firm where it should be firm. Her touch was alchemical, everywhere her fingers grazed his skin turning to fire.

She drew him backward with her, toward the bed, and together they fell onto the soft mattress in a tangle of arms and legs. He had just drawn his mouth away from hers to ask whether she was sure about what they were doing when the room went utterly black.

He froze, his pulse thundering in his ears. Except for their ragged breathing, there was no other sound to be heard, not even the ubiquitous hum of electricity through the wires.

*Come on, auxiliary power,* he thought. *Kick in. Please, kick in.*

But ten seconds passed and nothing happened.

"What is it?" Annie asked, her voice faint and trembling.

"I don't know," he admitted. "Auxiliary power should have kicked in after ten seconds." He rolled away from her and sat up, digging in his pocket for his flashlight. He ran it around the room until he spotted their supply bag and hurried to pull his Glock and holster from inside.

"What does it mean that it didn't?" she asked.

He strapped the gun to the waistband of his jeans and looked at her in the faint beam of his flashlight. She looked scared and vulnerable, and the urge to protect her at any cost gave fuel to his determination.

"Nothing good," he said.

## Chapter Fourteen

"Damn it." Wade shoved his cell phone into the pocket of his jeans. "Cell service is out."

"Blocked intentionally?" Annie felt herself skating precariously on the edge of panic. She had to keep herself together. If they were in as much danger as Wade clearly believed, he didn't need to be saddled with someone in full freak-out mode.

"Most likely." Wade edged his way to the door and opened it quickly, taking a peek outside. "We need to get to Jesse. He may know more about what's going on. Plus, safety in numbers."

She knew he was right. Whatever was going on outside, they were sitting ducks in here. On the move, they had half a chance to escape.

But even with Wade and his big black gun by her side as they crept out into the darkened corridor, Annie felt as if she wore a neon target on her back. There were no lights in the hallway, and very little ambient light bleeding through from the handful of rooms with open doors. Wade didn't seem fazed by the darkness, moving with unexpected grace down the hallway, sweeping the open rooms in search of lurking shadows and hidden threats. Encountering nothing on the current floor, they slipped into the stairwell at the end of the hall.

Wade wrapped his arm around her shoulders, holding her close. The heat of his body enveloped her, doing wonders for her shattered nerves. "Be still and quiet. Let's just listen."

Her heart was pounding too relentlessly in her ears for her to be able to hear much else, but Wade seemed satisfied, after a couple of moments, that they were alone in the stairwell. "Jesse's office is in the next building over. We need to go down two flights and then take the covered walkway to the main building."

He moved ahead slowly, leading with care as they descended two pitch-black flights of stairs. Reaching the door at the second landing, Wade paused, catching Annie's hand in his own. "Once we get out in the walkway, we'll be exposed. It's glassed in but not closed in. Anyone outside the building can see us moving. The glass is bullet-resistant, but—"

Her pulse notched up wildly. "Should we take it at a run?"

"If you're up to it, yeah. Not a bad idea." Wade pushed at the door but it didn't open.

"What's wrong?" Annie asked, her nerves rattling.

"Something's blocking the door." Wade pushed his shoulder against the door again, digging in harder. The door moved forward a few inches, allowing him room to slip through the narrow opening.

"Wait," he said as Annie followed him through the dark gap, but it was too late. Her foot caught on something just on the other side of the door and she sprawled forward, landing painfully hard on her side.

"Annie!" Wade's arms wrapped around her, tugging her close. "Are you okay?"

She felt something warm and wet beneath her hand. A metallic odor burned in her nose.

Blood.

She scrambled backward, out of Wade's grip, and rubbed her hand frantically against the nubby carpet. "Wade?" Her voice wavered.

She heard a soft snick and light glowed across the floor. A few feet in front of her, his body partially wedged against the door, lay a man in a dark blue security guard uniform. His head was twisted at an odd angle and blood pooled, crimson-black, around his upper torso.

"Who is it?" she breathed.

"Fiorello, one of the guards."

"Is he dead?" The question seemed stupid, considering how utterly dead the man looked.

"Yes." Wade reached her side and pulled her to her feet, wrapping his strong arm around her shoulder again. "Let's go find Jesse."

"Take it at a run?" she whispered, gazing at the long, dark corridor ahead. Glass encircled the top half of the tunnel, revealing a star-sprinkled night sky above and thick stands of trees on either side of the building.

Shooters could be standing behind any of those trees, she thought. She forced the image to the back of her mind, where she'd tucked her panic moments earlier.

They clasped hands and started running through the corridor, moving at a pace that felt entirely too slow for Annie. She could almost feel dozens of invisible eyes on them as they ran, gazing in through the fragile-looking glass bubble over their heads.

As they neared the far end of the corridor, a door opened and two dark figures glided into the corridor.

Wade stopped abruptly, pulling Annie behind him.

"Wade?"

Annie felt Wade's body relax. "Yeah. What's going on with the power?"

"Not sure." Jesse Cooper moved slowly toward them, a slim, dark-haired woman pulling up the rear. Annie couldn't make out much about her features, but there was something about her that seemed familiar.

"We just found Fiorello dead at the other end of the tunnel," Wade warned. "Looks like a gunshot wound to the throat."

Jesse muttered a low profanity. "Any sign of Hotchkiss or Fordham?"

"Not so far," Wade answered. "Can we get out of this shooting gallery and go somewhere covered?"

Jesse backed toward the door and led them into the main office building. "The backup generator never kicked in."

"I know." Wade kept his arm firmly around Annie's waist, the hard heat of his body a welcome distraction from her escalating fear. "I think we have to assume there are already bad guys inside the castle walls."

"Maybe just one," the dark-haired woman said quietly.

"He isn't working alone," Jesse disagreed. He turned on a flashlight, spreading a pale glow through the narrow corridor in which they now stood.

"Who isn't working alone?" Wade asked.

"Derek Fordham," Jesse answered. "Evie came across some discrepancies in his expense vouchers—"

*Evie,* Annie thought, finally placing the familiar-looking brunette. "Evie Marsh?"

Evie looked up at her, smiling slightly. "I wasn't sure you'd remember me. It's been a long time, and you always spent more time with Rita."

"We really need to talk to your father," Annie said flatly.

"I know. I've tried to talk to him but he shuts me out."

"Let's see if we can get to the vaults," Jesse interrupted. "It has an added layer of protection to work with."

"But no way out," Wade protested.

"You're not going to need a way out," Jesse said, already moving toward the stairwell at the end of the corridor. "I'm going to get out of here and get help. Your job is to stay here and keep Evie and Annie safe."

Annie felt Wade's body go tense beside her, though he said nothing aloud. She caught his hand in hers and gave it a strong squeeze.

His gaze shifted, locking with hers for a moment. She gazed up at him, infusing as much trust as she could in that one look. She was beginning to understand Wade Cooper, what he feared and what he needed. Right now, more than anything, he needed to believe in himself and his ability to keep them all safe.

"Okay," Wade said. "We'll stay here and hunker down."

"I need a weapon," Evie said.

Jesse looked doubtful. "Evie—"

"So help me, if you say I'm just an accountant one more time, I'm going to slug you." Evie's chin came up. "You're the one who decided to train clerks the same way you'd train field operatives. Let me do what I've learned."

"Okay." Jesse led them forward through the darkened corridors until he reached a room fitted with a large steel door and multiple locks. He pulled out a set of keys and opened the door, which led into a small vault stocked with a wide assortment of weapons.

"You have a preference?" Jesse asked Evie.

"How about that Kel-Tec compact?"

Jesse retrieved the compact pistol and a holster for her. He unlocked a drawer nearby and pulled out a couple of boxes of ammunition as well, handing them over to Evie to load the pistol.

Annie eyed the weapons on the wall, wondering if she would be more dangerous armed than not. She knew her way around a pistol; her father had taken her target shooting many times when she was younger and made sure she knew how to take care of a weapon, from cleaning it to shooting it. But living in D.C. for the past ten years, she hadn't spent much time around weapons. It had been a long time since she'd been target shooting.

"Do you know how to use a weapon?" Wade asked her quietly.

"Yes, but it's been a while."

"Would you feel safer armed?"

She looked up at him. "I feel safe with you."

His expression softened. "But would you feel even safer with a weapon?"

"I think I'd be better off without a weapon someone could take from me," she decided.

"That's settled, then," Jesse said. "I've got to get a move on."

"Be careful," Wade said as they walked with Jesse out of the armory into the corridor. "Don't play the hero—if you can't get out, get back here and cover your tail."

"I'll get out," Jesse said with confidence. Annie didn't know if he really believed what he was saying or if he'd gotten very good at pretending to be invulnerable. Either way, she found herself sharing his certainty that he'd find some way out of the complex.

But what happened then? If Jesse was right and the building was already under silent siege, would she, Evie and Wade become hostages in a deadly standoff?

"The vault is on the third floor," Wade murmured, leading them back into the stairwell.

"Is there a bathroom where I can wash the blood off my hands?" she asked.

He gave her a sympathetic look and led her back into the corridor. "Second door on the right."

She went inside the restroom and scrubbed her bloodstained hand clean, fighting a light wave of nausea. As she walked back out to where the others were waiting, she realized her legs were beginning to ache from all the walking, the burn in her muscles giving her an odd sense of déjà vu.

She'd been left standing for hours at a time early in her captivity, her hands tied to a hook overhead to keep her from sitting on the floor. Sleep had been next to impossible. Not that her captors had cared. Sleep deprivation had no doubt been part of their intent in keeping her from sitting or lying down. They'd wanted her broken. Malleable.

"Are you okay?" Wade asked as she reached them.

She nodded. "I was just remembering—they kept me on my feet for days. My leg muscles were jelly by the time they were done with me."

"I guess they're feeling pretty jelly-like at the moment, huh? All this running around."

She managed a soft huff of laughter. "Yeah. Feeling the burn."

"If it makes you feel any better," Evie said from behind them, a wry tone to her voice, "I'm feeling the burn a bit myself. "

"Just another flight to go." Wade led them back into the stairwell and headed upward. He was barely limping at all, Annie noticed with a secret smile. Maybe the chance to play the hero again had been all he really needed to push past the slowdown in his rehab.

They emerged from the stairwell into the pitch-black main corridor of the third floor. What little illumination twilight had shed on the darkened office had now died away, starlight too weak to offer more than the faintest break in the relentless gloom.

"Should we use the flashlight, or is it safer to stay dark?" Annie asked.

"We can use the flashlight once we're in the vault." Wade moved forward slowly, his hand sliding with a whisper of friction against the wall as he led the way. Annie stayed close to him, her hand curled in the tail of his T-shirt, while Evie brought up the rear.

They had made it almost halfway down the hallway when Annie heard a soft gasp behind her. She tugged Wade's shirt, halting him. "Evie?" she whispered.

There was the sound of a scuffle somewhere in the dark behind them. Wade whipped around and swung the flashlight up, the beam cutting through the darkness. The light caught Annie right in the eyes, contracting her pupils painfully and forcing her to shut her eyes against the brightness. Brilliant afterimages burned behind her eyelids as she groped closer to Wade.

"Don't move!" Wade called out, and as she felt his arm move upward, she realized he had pulled his weapon. Instinctively, she dropped to the floor, out of his field of fire.

There were more scuffling sounds down the hallway, including soft feminine grunts of effort and a distinctly masculine growl of pain. She peered down the hall, trying to make sense of the two shadows writhing together a few feet away in one of the open doorways.

Suddenly, one of the two shadows broke away from the other. Evie, Annie saw as the younger woman raced down the hallway toward them, her short legs churning.

Wade pulled both Evie and Annie behind him. "How many?" he asked.

"Just one. Male. I think he may have been wearing a ski mask or something over his face," Evie answered breathlessly. "He went into the IT unit—he's probably headed for the exit at the end of the hall."

Wade looked at them, clearly torn between going after the masked man and sticking close to Evie and Annie. He decided to stay put. "We'll never beat him to the exit." He placed his hand low on Annie's back, gently urging her down the hall ahead of him.

"Evie, you watch our backside. You held onto the Kel-Tec, didn't you?"

She showed him the compact pistol.

They inched up the hallway until they reached a large set of double doors. Wade turned the knob of the nearest door. It rattled uselessly in his hand, not budging.

"It's locked," he said. "It's never locked."

"Try the other doorknob," Evie suggested.

He did as she suggested, with similar results. "Locked tight."

"And you don't have a key?" Annie asked.

"It's never locked," he repeated, sounding frustrated.

"Can you pick it?" Evie suggested.

Wade pulled a small multiblade knife from his pocket. "Not my area of expertise, but I'll give it a try."

The tension coiled in Annie's gut tightened painfully as she watched Wade work at the lock. Despite his disclaimer, he seemed to know what he was doing. Within a couple of minutes, she heard an audible click from within the door latch, and the handle turned in Wade's hand.

He pushed open the door carefully, leading with his Glock. Evie edged forward, the Kel-Tec in hand as well, and together, she and Wade swept the room.

Annie stayed in the rear, the skin on her back rippling as if phantom fingers played across her flesh.

She darted a quick look down the hall behind her but saw nothing but a deep, black void.

"Is it clear?" she whispered.

"Sort of," Wade answered. He reached back and pulled her with him inside the room, closing the doors behind them. Evie's flashlight was on, painting the room with a narrow beam of light. Annie followed the beam to its end point and sucked in a quick, shocked gasp.

On the floor in front of a large steel door lay two crumpled bodies, both in uniform. Wade stepped forward, into the beam of light, and bent next to the bodies to check their pulses. He looked up at Evie and Annie, squinting against the beam of the flashlight. He shook his head. "Both dead."

Evie stepped closer, flashing the light beam on one of the two men. "Is that—?"

"Derek Fordham," Wade said with a nod.

"Was I wrong about him?" Evie asked, sounding horrified.

"Maybe not," Wade said. "Wouldn't be the first time bad guys turned on one of their own. Maybe he was a liability and they considered him expendable."

Annie moved closer to Wade, missing the solid heat of his body beside hers. He stood and wrapped his arm around her waist, as if reading her need in her expression.

She leaned against him, her heart pounding. "If

this was the mole in the company," she murmured, "and he's now dead, it means we don't even have a clue who we're up against now."

Evie and Wade both looked at her, their expressions grim.

She swallowed hard and asked the obvious question. "If there's another mole besides Fordham, how do we know who we can trust?"

## Chapter Fifteen

At least eight men created a perimeter outside the Cooper Security offices, by Jesse's count. He'd done a slow, thorough reconnaissance of the ground floor, keeping out of sight and listening hard for any sound that someone had breached the perimeter.

If anyone had, it could be no more than one person, maybe two. A larger force would have inevitably made more noise.

The office building Jesse had helped design and build for the company wasn't set up like a fortress, though there were multiple alarm systems that, in most cases, would have alerted him to problems before they started happening. But clearly, he'd somehow allowed a spy—possibly more than one—into the company, and there were consequences to his lack of judgment. When things were back under control, he'd take a long, hard look at their vetting process and other internal security procedures, but for now, self-recriminations were an unneeded distraction.

He'd screwed up. The situation had turned into an unholy mess. And the only way to fix any of it before things deteriorated any further was to get out of here and go for help.

There wasn't some super-secret exit to the Cooper Security office building, but that didn't mean there weren't ways to get out without being seen. The underground parking deck, where they kept their fleet of specialty vehicles when they weren't in use, had an unobtrusive ground level door that led directly into the woods behind the office. The exit wasn't marked in any way that would have drawn the attention of the intruders, and only a small handful of Cooper Security agents knew anything about the door, which had been put there mostly to allow deep cover agents to move in and out of the building without being seen by others.

There had been only a few such instances of that kind of undercover operation in the four years of Cooper Security's existence. The company tended to specialize in more open security assignments, where a strong and visible presence served as a preventive measure against bad acts. So as far as Jesse knew, Derek Fordham would have had no reason to know anything about the side exit. Jesse just hoped he hadn't learned about it from someone else.

The door had an automatic lock, but Jesse had

the keys to every lock in the place. He searched his bulky key ring until he found the small key that opened the side door. He pulled out his SIG Sauer P220 and checked the magazine, reassuring himself that he had all eight rounds—plus one in the chamber—at his disposal if he needed them.

*Deep breath. Focus.*

He unlocked the door and opened it slowly. Carefully.

Outside, the woods were still, not even a light breeze stirring the leafy canopy overhead. The warm temperature of the afternoon had faded to a faint, autumnal coolness that heralded the coming winter. In a couple of months, the nights would be cold and often dank. There might even be the threat of an early snow.

But not tonight.

He slipped through the door and eased outside, keeping his eyes and ears open for any movement. The ground floor of the parking deck jutted out into the woods on this side, with no real clearing to separate it from the natural woodlands that surrounded it. So when Jesse let the door fall locked behind him, he was standing in the woods, surrounded by pines, hickories and oaks that created a tall shelter from the rest of the property.

Would the S.S.U. have posted people in the woods around the building? If they were smart, they would, but he also knew that the S.S.U. had figured out long ago that there was almost no way to beat a Cooper in these woods. Jesse, his siblings and his cousins had all grown up here, schooled in woodland tracking by some of the best trackers the county had to offer—their own fathers.

The S.S.U. had learned not to challenge the Coopers in the woods. So maybe he had a chance of getting out of here and finding backup before things went belly-up inside.

He wished he could call Wade and find out what was going on. For all he knew, the S.S.U. agents flanking Cooper Security had already started their assault on the building. His brother, Annie and Evie could be under siege right this very moment.

*Can't think about it. Got to get help.*

Jesse forced his thoughts away from the ones he'd left behind and concentrated on moving silently through the woods, heading inexorably east. He'd reach County Road 17 soon. A half mile down the road, there was a gas station with a pay phone out front.

Furtive sounds of movement to his immediate west froze him in place. Jesse slowed his breathing, concentrating on getting his heart rate down. Sheltered under the low-hanging limbs of a magnolia tree, he'd be hard to spot as long as he stood still.

A shadow glided through the woods, making only a little noise. But it was enough for Jesse to easily track the black-clad figure's forward movement. He waited until the shadowy figure moved out of sight before he restarted his trek east toward the road.

If this was the S.S.U.—and Jesse couldn't imagine who else would have the audacity or skill to try to pull a siege on Cooper Security—they were taking a lot of chances trying to get their hands on Annie Harlowe.

How much did the general's daughter know about her father's secrets?

"It's not opening." Wade's voice darkened with frustration. "The lock is electrical."

"And there's usually backup power," Evie murmured.

Annie slumped back against the wall, her legs feeling suddenly weak and shaky. The darkness surrounding them seemed bigger than the faint beam of light shining from Wade's flashlight. It devoured the light, filling the rest of the room with dancing shadows that swamped Annie with a stifling sense of déjà vu.

Small room. No light, little sound except the ragged cadence of her own breathing and swishing thud of her pulse in her ears.

*Don't panic. Don't let them see your fear.*

She knew they were watching her. They were always watching, their malevolent regard tangible as a cold touch.

They timed their interrogations so carefully, probing when she felt her weakest. And maybe if she'd been a different sort of person, their tactic might have worked on her. But she was her father's daughter in one significant way: she'd inherited his massive stubborn streak. Having her mysterious captors try to play on her emotions, her weaknesses, merely served to stoke her anger to fiery heights.

They'd gotten nowhere with her. Not a single one of her father's secrets had slipped past her lips in the three weeks they'd held her captive.

The cold, black room faded into the larger, airier room that housed the Cooper Security vault. Wade and Evie still huddled around the closed vault door, heads close as they discussed how to get inside.

"If it's electronic, I don't know that there's a non-electronic way to access it," Evie said flatly.

"I can't believe Jesse didn't think of that before he left," Wade growled.

"I think he was mostly concentrating on how to get out of here safely," Evie defended.

"I hope he did," Wade murmured. "He may be our only hope now."

"Is the vault the only safe place to hide?" Annie asked.

Wade and Evie both turned to look at her. "It's the safest," Wade said flatly. "The vault lock is coded, and only a small handful of people know the code. All family."

*All trusted, in other words,* Annie thought. "But knowing the code is useless if you don't have a way to use it."

Wade's eyes narrowed suddenly. "Right."

Annie pushed herself away from the wall and approached him, reading the flash of comprehension evident in his dark eyes. "What are you thinking?"

"Why do you suppose the guards were in here in the first place?" He waved his hand at the two dead guards.

"I don't know," Annie answered, trying to follow the flow of his thoughts. "Maybe they were trying to find a way into the vault?"

"Would either of them have the code?" Evie asked.

"No." Wade shook his head firmly. "Only family members have the code. But maybe Fordham didn't know that."

"Maybe he thought Hotchkiss knew?" Evie asked.

"Maybe. Or maybe he was planning to use Hotchkiss to lure one of the family up here." Wade's forehead creased. "Though I can't explain how both of them ended up dead."

"What if they killed each other?" Evie suggested.

Annie followed Wade's gaze as it settled on the bodies. The dead men lay as they'd found them when they entered the room, close to each other but not touching. Slowly, Wade leaned over and moved his flashlight beam over the scene.

"Both men's guns were drawn," he said aloud. He hunkered down by the closest of the two bodies. "Either of you have a pen on you?"

Annie didn't, but Evie pulled a pen out of the bag slung over her shoulder. Wade took it and carefully picked up the pistol lying on the floor by the closest body. He drew it close and gave a sniff. "Might have been discharged." He pulled a dark blue handkerchief from his back pocket and held the gun with it while he checked the magazine. "Two rounds missing."

He checked the other body, the one Evie had called Fordham. The mole, or so they'd thought. "One round discharged. I guess they might have shot each other."

"So Hotchkiss was trying to keep Fordham out of the vault? Maybe he stumbled on Fordham trying to get inside?"

"Maybe they're not here because of me at all," Annie said aloud.

Wade looked at her. "We can't assume anything."

"But they were trying to get into the vault. Maybe what they really want is inside there," Evie suggested.

Annie could tell by the look on Wade's face that there was something inside the vault the S.S.U.

would definitely want to get their hands on. She had a sinking feeling she knew what it was. "The journal is in there, isn't it?"

Wade's eyes locked with Annie's, and she saw the answer.

"What journal?" Evie asked.

Wade looked at her. "That's a question for your father, I'm afraid. If you can ever get him to talk to you."

Evie's lips pressed to a thin line. "He's avoiding me these days. All he's willing to talk about is Rita's wedding. Anytime I bring up anything else, he closes off."

"He's scared," Annie said gently, feeling sorry for the younger woman. She couldn't imagine how frustrated she'd feel if her father was so actively keeping dangerous secrets from her instead of sharing them, as her own father had done.

Yes, she was in more danger than she might have been in had her father kept his secret to himself. But she was also empowered by the knowledge he'd shared with her. She could actively do something to thwart a group of very bad people planning very bad things.

She hoped she'd get a chance to thank her father for his trust.

"I don't care how scared he is," Evie growled. "Keeping secrets from us just makes us more vulnerable. He thinks he can protect us from everything, but how can he do that if we don't have the necessary facts? We have to be able to act in our own defense as well."

"Tell her about the journal," Annie told Wade.

He gazed back at her, his eyes dark with hesitation. "I can't."

"It's her secret, too," Annie said flatly, moving closer. "Evie's part of this, whether she wants to be or not. The people after the journal have already proved they're willing to use family members as leverage. Evie needs to know what kind of trouble may be out there for her."

"You're scaring me," Evie said in a hushed voice.

"There's a coded journal in the safe," Wade said after a brief pause. "It belonged to an army general named Edward Ross."

"I knew General Ross," Evie said. "At least, I knew of him. He and my dad were friends."

"My father was a friend of General Ross, too," Annie said. "You know he died a few months ago."

Evie nodded. "We went to the funeral."

"We don't think his car crash was an accident," Wade said.

Annie looked up with surprise. "You think he was killed?"

"I think at first they thought eliminating the three generals would solve the problem."

"What's the problem, exactly?" Evie asked.

"The coded journal contains a narrative," Wade

said. "It outlines the suspicions of the three generals about a far-reaching conspiracy that goes pretty high in the government."

"What kind of conspiracy?" Evie asked.

"We're not sure," Wade answered. "We think it probably has something to do with some of the things Barton Reid was doing over the past few years."

"It's bigger than that," Annie said, overcome by the sudden realization.

Wade's gaze snapped around to meet hers. "Do you know something?"

She nodded, the memory flooding in to fill some of the empty spaces left in her mixed-up brain. "I can't remember everything—I'm not sure my dad really told me everything—but I think it has something to do with an international consortium of think tanks, world leaders and global business leaders. Something to do with oil."

"A cartel like OPEC?"

She shook her head. "No, not like that. More like—I don't know how to describe it exactly." Her head was beginning to ache with the strain of trying to remember. "I get the sense that they want to control petroleum production and treat oil as a global resource so that a small group of countries no longer controls the entire world's energy reserves."

"Wealth redistribution?" Evie asked. "Not exactly a novel idea."

"It's not just the wealth." Annie shook her head. "Although I can't pretend that's not a big part of it. But it's also about controlling the resources so that winners and losers aren't left up to the market."

"I could see where a lot of countries—hell, a lot of people across the globe—might find such a thing tempting. No more having to deal with desert dictators in order to get your hands on enough energy to run your own country? It sounds good on paper," Wade said. "But you're just trading one dictator for another, really."

"Exactly. But if there are people in our government willing to put their power and resources behind the idea—"

"And there would be," Evie said bleakly. "There's always someone in government looking for a way to gain more control over the rest of the world. That's why they went into politics in the first place."

"Espera," Annie said, the word popping into her head. "That's what they call themselves. The Espera Group."

Wade shook his head. "Never heard of them."

"Me, either," Evie admitted.

"I hadn't, either, but my dad told me that's who they think is behind this push for regulation."

"What else did he tell you about the group?" Wade asked.

Annie pressed her fingertips to her forehead. "I'm not sure. I'm only remembering things in bits and pieces."

Wade crossed to her side, wrapping his arm around her shoulder and pulling her closer. "Don't push yourself. What you've already remembered is so much more than we knew before."

"I wonder if Jesse's ever heard about the Espera Group," Evie murmured. "He's usually so tuned in to what's going on in the world."

"He may have heard of them," Wade admitted, "but if he had any idea they might be connected to the coded journal, he never let on."

"Would he have?" Annie asked.

"I think so." Wade lifted his hand to cradle her cheek. "You look tired."

She felt tired. All the running around Cooper Security had taken a toll on her still-depleted energy. "I'm running on empty," she admitted.

"Maybe we should find somewhere to hunker down and hide until Jesse comes back with reinforcements," Evie suggested. She sounded confident, Annie thought, as if she were utterly certain Jesse would come back with the cavalry to their rescue.

Annie hoped Evie was right. She hoped Jesse could come through for them. But as long as she had Wade on her side, she thought, she liked her odds right where she was.

"You need to rest a little longer?" Wade asked, his fingers lingering on her cheek.

"No, let's go." She forced herself to step away from his touch, though she could think of nothing she wanted more than to stay right there, his body so close she could feel its heat and power, his fingers touching her, reminding her of both his gentleness and strength.

She hadn't needed another person in a long, long time. Her parents had taught her how to be independent and self-sufficient. Part of it had been a protective measure to help her deal with the constant moves and her father's perpetual absences. Part of it had been an acknowledgment, she thought, of her own personality. She made a point of not needing other people because needing people was too limiting. It crowded her life, cramped her style, held her back from the things she wanted to accomplish.

But, God help her, she was beginning to think she needed Wade Cooper. Even stepping away from him a couple of feet, letting cool air replace the heat that had flowed between them when he stood closer, made her ache as if she'd just torn a piece of herself away.

"Any ideas where we should go next?" Evie asked.

"I was thinking maybe the infirmary. It's on the second floor, so we'll still have a little warning if intruders try to enter. It also has beds, so we can rest a little while. And there are scalpels and other tools we can use as weapons if we need them."

Evie nodded. "Good choice."

"I'll take the lead. Can you bring up the rear?" He moved forward, catching Annie's elbow in his hand. "Just downstairs one flight and we'll have to walk to the other end of the hallway, but that's it. Then you can rest."

His hand felt warm and firm around her elbow, She took a shaky breath, both alarmed and thrilled by how powerfully his touch affected her.

Did he feel the same thing when she touched him?

He let her go, and she bit her lip to keep from groaning. "I'll go ahead to the stairwell, make sure everything's clear. Y'all stay back about twenty yards until I give you a signal to join me, okay?"

Annie nodded, and next to her, Evie murmured, "Okay."

Wade moved ahead, his flashlight beam painting dancing shadows across the walls of the corridor. He cut the light when he reached the stairwell and the darkness swallowed him.

"I can't see anything," Annie whispered to Evie. Evie didn't respond.

"Evie?"

There was a soft moan somewhere behind her, but she couldn't see anything in the dark void behind her.

She reached out her hand, feeling for the wall. Her fingers connected with something solid.

And alive.

"Evie?" she whispered, even though the wall of muscle beneath her fingers couldn't possibly belong to a woman's body.

Her eyes had begun adjusting to the darkness, enough that she caught the faintest glint of light on metal rising over her in the darkness.

A needle. She knew it bone deep, at the quivering core of her hidden fear. The men who'd taken her had loved their needles, whether they delivered pain or oblivion.

She could feel the straps on her arms, holding her in place. Smelled the fear rising off her skin like heat.

The needle hovered over her, cool gray eyes locked with hers as the man behind the mask contemplated his task at hand.

He enjoyed it, she realized. He liked the way it made him feel, wielding the needle and delivering pain or relief according to his own whims.

To hell with that.

She pushed away from him as he started to bring the needle down, almost getting away. But he caught her arm, jerking her back toward him.

"No!" she cried, kicking blindly at his legs.

A beam of light washed over them, illuminating the face of her captor. She gazed up, expecting to see the familiar black hood and balaclava, concealing all but those cold, gray eyes.

But the face of her captor was uncovered. Straight, ordinary features filled an unremarkable face. Only the lethal light in his storm-cloud eyes distinguished him in any way.

Still, she realized with surprise, she'd seen him before. Not just behind a black mask in some secret torture chamber but out in the open. He'd been smiling at her that time, his eyes kind rather than cruel.

In the hospital, she remembered suddenly. He'd been the attending physician at Chickasaw County Hospital. He'd examined her right there in her hospital room, pretending he had her best interests at heart.

"Dr. Ambrose," she said aloud.

His gray eyes crinkled at the corners, and he jerked her around until her back was pressed against his chest. She felt the prick of the needle in her skin and gasped.

A pinpoint of light shone from the end of the hallway, forcing her to squint. She heard footsteps and the guttural growl of a man enraged.

"Let her go, or I'll kill you where you stand," Wade commanded.

## Chapter Sixteen

The tip of the needle lay next to Annie's carotid artery, separated by only a thin layer of flesh. Already, Wade could see a droplet of dark red staining her pale skin where the tip of the needle had pricked her neck.

The man wielding the needle squinted against the beam of Wade's flashlight, but he didn't let Annie go. He looked familiar, Wade thought, but he couldn't quite place him.

Wade leveled the Glock at the man's head. "Put the needle down," he growled, his pulse pounding in his ears. "Put it down and let her go."

"That's not going to happen," the man answered, and it was the sound of his voice that clicked Wade's memory into place.

The doctor from the hospital. Dr. Ambrose. The one who'd ordered Wade out of Annie's room so he could check her over.

The needle in his hand seemed suddenly more lethal than ever.

"You won't get out of here alive if you do anything to her," Wade warned, keeping his fear in check and giving free rein to his rage. He couldn't afford to let any weakness show, no matter how badly his knees were shaking at the sight of Annie in danger.

He had to get her out of this. She'd trusted him to protect her, and that was what he was going to do, no matter what it took.

If he had to shoot the man between the eyes to make him let go of the needle, he'd do it.

"Where's Evie?" Annie asked, her voice tight with fear.

"She won't be waking up anytime soon," Ambrose responded, pulling Annie more firmly in front of him. She was too close now, Wade thought with frustration. He should have taken the shot a moment ago, when she was farther out of his line of fire.

"What's in the syringe?"

"Enough tranquilizer to stop her heart," Ambrose answered flatly. "So it's very important that you don't try to stop me. One push of this plunger and it's over."

"You hurt her, I kill you."

"Yeah, I'm aware of the consequences. But I'm betting you'd rather let me take her out of here alive, right? You're not going to let her die just so you can take a shot at me. You Coopers don't roll like that."

"You don't know anything about us Coopers."

"Let him take me," Annie said. "I don't think he's bluffing about what's in the syringe."

Wade was sure he wasn't. "I can't let him take you out of here."

Annie stared at him, her dark eyes glittering in the beam of the flashlight. Suddenly, her eyes rolled back in her head and she sagged against the doctor, catching him off guard.

Wade held his breath, his eyes on the tip of the needle. It pushed a little deeper into her neck but Ambrose had to let the syringe go to keep Annie's deadweight from dragging him down.

Suddenly, Annie jerked away from the doctor's grasp and rolled away, leaving Wade with an open shot at the doctor.

Ambrose looked up at Wade, his eyes wide with fear. Wade steadied his Glock until Ambrose's forehead was in his crosshairs. "Stand up and put your hands behind your head."

Ambrose stood up slowly, lifting his hands and clasping them behind his head. He shot a wry smile at Wade, his jaw muscle working furiously.

Suddenly, his whole body went rigid, and he fell to the ground, convulsing violently.

Keeping the gun and flashlight trained on Ambrose's jerking body, Wade called out for Annie.

"I'm okay." She scrambled toward him, just outside the beam of the flashlight. "I faked a flashback."

"Get behind me." He wasn't sure what was happening to Ambrose, though he had a sinking suspicion he knew what the convulsions were about.

Annie circled behind him, her hands pressing firm and flat against his back. "What's happening to him?"

"Not sure," Wade admitted, waiting out the convulsions. If he was right, nothing he could do at this point would make a difference, and if he was wrong, he didn't want to walk into Ambrose's trap.

"Do you see Evie?" Annie whispered. "I thought I heard her moan—"

Ambrose's body fell still and silent. Taking a chance, Wade swept his flashlight away from Ambrose until the beam settled on a crumpled form a few feet behind the man's body. Evie, he realized, his heart sinking quickly until he saw she was stirring, trying to sit up.

"Don't try to move, Evie. Just stay where you are a second." Wade reached behind him and caught one of Annie's hands. "Stay right here. I'm going to check on him, but if he makes any move at all, I want you to run. Understand?"

"I won't leave you," she said in a low, strangled voice.

"You have to."

"Just check on him. And be careful."

Wade kept his Glock steady as he approached Ambrose's still body. He ran the flashlight beam over the body, looking for any signs of movement or life, but he was utterly still. Flecks of foam coated Ambrose's lips, Wade saw. He wasn't surprised. He'd seen this kind of reaction before.

He kicked away the syringe and bent carefully to check Ambrose's pulse. He didn't drop his guard, not even when he failed to detect a flutter of a heartbeat on either side of the man's neck.

He backed away slowly. "He's dead."

"How?" Annie asked.

"Cyanide pill," he answered tightly, remembering the man's smile and the way his jaw muscles had worked rapidly once Wade had him firmly in his gun sights. He must have had a capsule already in his mouth, in case he got caught. Wade had seen another S.S.U. operative take the same way out rather than risk being interrogated.

Maybe it was time to rethink just what kind of mercenaries they were up against. Most of the mercenaries Wade had ever come across were all about saving their own skins. They weren't suicide bombers.

They didn't take one for the team.

He searched Ambrose's pockets, procuring a small Smith & Wesson pistol and, more importantly, the safety cap for the syringe he'd used to threaten Annie. Wade put the cap on the syringe and shoved it into the pocket of his jacket. He'd have someone analyze the contents later.

"Evie, how're you doing?"

Evie sat up slowly, holding her head. "He cold-cocked me," she muttered, sounding furious.

"You sure he didn't inject you with anything?"

"No, he definitely hit me. Felt like he separated my head from my neck." She groaned as she slowly, unsteadily made her way to a standing position. She had to put her hand on the wall to stay upright. "I didn't even hear him coming, damn it."

"Don't kick yourself about it," Annie said. She tugged Wade's hand. "We need to get to the infirmary for sure, now."

Keeping himself between Annie and Ambrose's body, Wade hurried with her to Evie's side, helping the young accountant hobble past the body on the way to the stairs. "Sure you can make it to the infirmary?" he asked Evie.

"Yeah. My head's starting to clear already." She seemed to be steadier on her feet, Wade saw with relief. It was already going to be hard enough to explain to Jesse how he'd let Rita Marsh's little sister get coldcocked by an intruder without having to explain a coma as well.

They made it inside the stairwell and started downward, Wade keeping one hand on Evie's arm to make sure she didn't stumble and fall. They'd reached the midfloor landing when an ominous sound rose from the ground level.

Someone had opened the first floor door. Seconds later, the clatter of footsteps echoed up the stairwell.

Son of a bitch. He doused his flashlight immediately.

"Wade—" Annie's voice was barely a breath, but her grip was strong as she dug her fingers into his upper arm.

"I hear them," he answered just as quietly. "Up. We go up."

He gave Evie an upward push, half hauling her up the stairs to the second floor landing. He thought for a moment about detouring back down the second floor corridor, but they'd be easier targets out in an open hallway than moving upwards in the stairwell, where the stairs and railings would provide at least a modest amount of cover.

"How far up?" Evie whispered.

"To the roof," he answered, hoping he wasn't making an irrevocable mistake.

There was no way to make a silent approach, not in a Bell 407 helicopter. And there was always the risk of taking ground fire, but it was a chance Jesse thought was worth taking. The Bell was fitted with a thermal imager—something the pilot, Jesse's cousin J.D. Cooper, had talked Jesse into adding when they first started talking about using the Bell for fugitive tracking. Thermal imaging would give them their best overall look at the number of operatives they were up against at Cooper Security.

The first pass overhead sent heat signatures scattering for cover, but they escaped without taking any fire from the ground. "I saw ten operatives outside," J.D. said from the cockpit seat. "Could you see anyone inside?"

"I saw a blob of heat signatures on the eastern side of the building," Jesse answered, trying to picture the building's layout. On the eastern side of the building was one of the stairwells leading from the ground floor to the roof. "Maybe several people on the stairs."

Including Wade and the women?

"Let's take another pass," J.D. suggested.

Jesse braced himself for ground fire as the bird circled over the woods and headed back toward the Cooper Security complex. There were now six heat signatures outside the building, and the glowing blob in the eastern stairwell seemed to have grown in size. "I think they're heading up the stairs."

"No sign of Wade or the others?"

"I think they may be in the stairwell, too," Jesse said, tamping down a gut-load of fear.

J.D. muttered a low profanity. "When they reach the roof, they'll have nowhere else to run."

"So let's give them a way out," Jesse said, waving toward the heliport on the western edge of the roof. "Set down, and I'll give you cover fire." He left the copilot's seat and steadied himself next to the side door, bracing himself for the set down.

The helicopter lowered carefully to the helipad, buffeted by a light crosswind that nearly threw Jesse from his feet. He gripped the door tightly to hold himself steady, keeping his balance when the helicopter set down on the hard surface of the helipad. He opened the door and used it as cover as he aimed his SIG toward the roof door to the east.

WADE WAS MOVING FAST, keeping Evie on her feet and pulling Annie behind to keep them all together. If he was losing steam, he didn't show it, Annie thought with a mixture of admiration and frustration. For her part, she could use a rest, but she knew they didn't have the luxury of taking a break.

They had already passed the third floor landing. If her impression of the Cooper Security building layout was correct, their next stop would be the roof.

And then they'd really be sitting ducks.

As they neared the half landing, she heard the sound of an engine, impossibly loud and getting louder. Wade's hand gripped hers more tightly, a soft huff of laughter escaping his throat.

"It's a bird," he whispered in her ear.

"A helicopter?"

"Yep." He tugged her up the stairs more quickly. "And if it's who I think it is, the cavalry has arrived."

"The helipad's on the opposite side of the roof," Evie muttered, sounding despondent.

"We'll have to make a run for it."

Annie's lungs were already close to bursting as it was, but she dug deep, remembering the look in her father's eyes as he realized they were about to be taken. The memory was as clear and fully formed, frozen in her mind like a fly in amber.

*Protect the code,* her father had told her, seconds before the men in black had swept them into captivity.

She had no way of knowing whether or not her father had survived their abduction, but she had. And she knew her father's part of the code.

Whatever it took, she had to survive to protect the code.

They reached the roof door and burst through in a rush, cool wind ruffling past them with surprising strength. "There it is!" Wade growled, waving toward the red helicopter perched on the helipad at the opposite end of the roof. "Run for it?"

He kept her hand in his grasp, his other hand hooked in the crook of Evie's arm. Suddenly, a figure started running toward them from the helicopter, brandishing a weapon. In the few seconds it took to recognize Jesse Cooper, Annie's heart skipped about a half dozen beats.

She heard sound from behind them, the clatter of a door slamming open and footsteps racing behind them.

"Go, go, go!" That was Jesse's voice, loud and getting closer. He swung wide, around them, and started firing off shots.

Annie scrambled to keep pace with Wade as they raced for the helicopter. Wade shoved Evie inside first and turned, lifting Annie off her feet and setting her inside, as well.

As she crouched behind one of the seats, Wade disappeared from her sight, and she heard a fresh volley of gunfire join Jesse's fusillade of bullets.

"Wade!" she cried out, her heart in her throat.

"Stay down!" called a deep voice from the cockpit of the helicopter, barely audible over the roar of the engine.

Suddenly, two silhouettes filled the open doorway of the helicopter. They dived aboard and one of them slammed the door shut.

"Go, go, go!" That was Wade's voice, close enough that Annie couldn't stop herself from reaching out to touch him.

His fingers tangled with hers as he scrambled to her side. He wrapped his arms around her, pulling her close. "You okay?"

The helicopter lurched upward, throwing her

hard against Wade's side. He braced his legs against the seats in front of them, keeping her steady as the bird rose into the sky.

The sound of gunfire coincided with a couple of alarming pings of metal on metal. Wade wrapped himself more tightly around her, and she pressed her face against his neck, terror stealing her breath.

It seemed to be forever later before she heard someone call out, "We're clear. Buckle in!"

Wade pushed to his feet and helped her into the seat next to him. His hands shook a little as he fastened her seat belt around her.

Across from them, Jesse had helped Evie into the seat beside him and was examining her head injury with a dark scowl on his face.

"It's just a bump," she said, but her reassurance didn't seem to lighten Jesse's black mood a bit. He waved at the headsets hanging over the backs of the seats and put his own set on. Evie did the same.

Once Wade and Annie had their headsets on, Jesse spoke into the mike, his voice coming clear and hard across the headset speakers.

"What the hell happened in there?" he asked Wade.

"Long story," Wade spoke into the mike of his own headset, sounding weary for the first time. He threaded his fingers through Annie's, locking his gaze with hers as if the rest of the world around them had disappeared. "Get us to a safe place and I promise, we'll tell you all about it."

Annie darted a quick look at Jesse and found him still scowling at his brother. But if Wade noticed, he gave no sign of it, his attention focused on Annie's face, as if searching for reassurance that she was unhurt. She squeezed his hand.

"There are at least a dozen men inside or surrounding the perimeter of Cooper Security," Jesse said. "The Chickasaw County SWAT team and the Maybridge Police Emergency Services Unit are both heading to the scene."

Wade looked at his brother. "Could be a bloodbath."

"They know what they're up against," Jesse said. "They'll retreat if it gets too hairy—we've already called in Cooper Security reinforcements. All our best-trained field agents are already on the way there."

"We should go back and help," Evie said.

"No," Jesse said firmly. "You're injured, and Annie isn't trained for this kind of skirmish."

"We'll get the two of you somewhere safe and go back to swell the ranks," Wade said firmly.

Annie tightened her grip on Wade's hand. "You can't go back there."

He kissed her knuckles, his eyes dark with regret. "It's my job."

"Isabel's shoring up the perimeter security for

her farmhouse—that's where we're taking Annie and Evie," Jesse said. "Izzy, Ben, Mcgan and Evan will guard them until we can arrange something more permanent."

Annie looked at Wade with alarm. Something more permanent? Were they talking about sending her away somewhere, separating her from everything familiar to her?

Separating her from Wade?

There was no time to ask questions for the rest of the ride, as Wade and Jesse ended up discussing strategy back and forth over the headsets. Annie finally made herself take off the headset to tune them out, as the threat assessments they were throwing around were dire enough to scare the life out of her.

She had to believe Wade would be okay. He and the Cooper Security crew would round up the intruders and deliver them to the authorities without any more bloodshed.

It had to happen that way. Wade had to come back safely to her.

The helicopter landed on the road in front of a sprawling farmhouse in the middle of nowhere, the pilot managing to stay clear of the trees that flanked the road on both sides. As soon as they touched down, Jesse and Wade hurried the two women out of the helicopter and into the house, where Isabel and her husband, Ben, were waiting to take over.

"Wait!" Annie called as she realized Wade was heading right back out to the helicopter.

Wade turned to look at her, a question in his dark eyes.

She found herself at a loss for words to express the terror expanding in her chest like a poisonous cloud, making her sick with worry. She had no words for what she was feeling, no way to tell Wade just how scared she was at the thought of never seeing him again.

He crossed to her side, pulling her away from the others. "Don't be scared. Everything's going to be okay."

"You don't know that," she whispered.

He cradled her face between his big hands. "You'll be safe here. Isabel and Megan won't let anything happen to you."

"I'm not afraid for myself," she said bleakly. "I'm afraid for you. Going back there, dealing with those monsters—"

"We've dealt with them before. We know what we're doing."

Frustration with his blasé confidence filled her aching chest. "Famous last words, Cooper."

He smiled. "Try not to worry."

She grimaced. "Impossible."

"I'll be careful."

"You'd better." She closed her hands over his

where they lay on her face. "You come back alive, you hear me?"

A smile curved his lips. "That's usually the plan."

"I mean it, Wade."

His eyes glittered with amusement. She didn't know whether to smack him or kiss him. "So, is that an order?"

She nodded, her heart in her throat. "Yes. It is."

"Okay, then," he said, his smile spreading. "You're the boss."

"Say it," she demanded, needing to hear the words.

He dipped his head toward hers, brushing his lips lightly across her mouth. "I'll come back to you alive," he vowed.

She prayed he would be able to keep the promise.

WADE'S COUSIN AARON MET Jesse, Wade and about two-thirds of the active Cooper Security field agents at the edge of the perimeter the Chickasaw County SWAT team had formed around the Cooper Security office building. Dressed in body armor and a black helmet emblazoned with the Chickasaw County Sheriff's Department insignia, Aaron looked formidable as he broke away from a cluster of similarly dressed deputies and crossed to greet Wade, Jesse and the other Coopers who'd arrived to provide backup.

"The building is secure," he told them, but his

grim expression made Wade's gut tighten with dread.

"What aren't you telling me?"

"Well, for one thing, there are only two bodies in the building. Fiorello and Hotchkiss. No sign of Fordham or Dr. Ambrose. No sign of anyone else."

"They didn't want to leave any evidence behind," Jesse growled. "Damn it."

Wade's brother Rick muttered a string of low curses. "How'd they get away so quickly?"

"I think once Wade, Annie and Evie escaped their clutches, they lost their reason for being there," Aaron suggested.

"They couldn't get into the vault, which is where they probably assume the coded journal is," Jesse said. "Smarter to cut their losses and bug out as quickly as they could."

"Regroup and attack another day." Wade grimaced.

Jesse's cell phone rang and he excused himself to take the call. Rick put his hand on Wade's shoulder, giving it a squeeze. "I talked to Isabel a few minutes ago. Annie's fine. She's just worried about you." Rick gave him a knowing look. "She seems like a good woman. You could do worse."

"Marriage has made you soft, Rick," Wade shot back with a grin.

"Wade!" Jesse hurried toward him, pocketing

his phone. His grim expression made Wade's chest tighten with alarm.

"What is it?"

"Just got off the phone with Maddox Heller," Jesse said. Heller, Wade had learned recently, was Jesse's silent partner at Cooper Security. A former Marine security guard who'd funneled his unexpected inheritance into Jesse's start-up security firm, Heller had an expansive network of contacts in the intelligence services, including the CIA.

"What did he want?" Wade asked.

"He just received word that Emmett Harlowe just showed up in the E.R. at Chickasaw County Hospital. Alive and well."

## Chapter Seventeen

The safe house was a nondescript, brick and clapboard ranch-style house in the middle of an ordinary suburban neighborhood just north of Birmingham, Alabama. It had a large, fenced-in backyard, a wide, grassy front lawn and a side yard amply sheltered by dogwood and hickory trees.

Annie arrived around ten that morning, accompanied by a pair of Cooper Security agents she'd met briefly outside a truck stop a couple of days earlier. Delilah Hammond, the female agent, looked a bit more put-together and dangerous than she had when she was pretending to be Annie. She was definitely all business. Troy Cooper, Wade's cousin, was more easygoing and quick with a smile. Annie found herself gravitating toward him, and not just because she hoped he might tell her why she'd been spirited away from Isabel Scanlon's house and taken on a two-hour, twisty and circuitous drive to this safe house.

"What's going to happen next?" she asked Troy as she settled at the kitchen table across from him. Nearby, Delilah was watching the street outside the house through the square window set in the patio door.

"Two more people will be joining us, along with a few more guards," Troy answered.

"Well, that's vague."

Delilah looked over her shoulder. "It's supposed to be. Mission integrity is vital."

"And you think I'm going to spill some top secret? To whom?"

"She has a point, Dee."

Delilah shot a pointed look at Troy. "They'll be here soon. Everything will make sense then."

Annie snapped her mouth shut to keep from saying something rude to Delilah. The woman was putting her life on the line to protect her, after all.

But did she have to be so damned annoying about it?

"Why didn't you let me wait to talk to Wade?"

"We had to move fast," Delilah answered. Her back went suddenly rigid, and her hand moved to the Glock tucked into her waistband holster.

Troy stood and joined her at the window, his posture equally tense. Then he relaxed visibly and turned to look at Annie. "Here we go."

Annie rose to her feet, trying to see past them

through the small window, but the two agents blocked her view completely. Frustrated, she dropped back into her chair and waited for whatever was going to happen next.

The agents stepped back from the door, Troy pulling it open to admit their new visitors. Annie didn't know what to expect, but the person she saw standing in the doorway caught her utterly by surprise.

"Daddy?"

Emmett Harlowe's dark eyes locked with his daughter's, and he started to laugh a low, hearty chuckle that did more to relieve Annie's fears than anything she'd heard in a long time.

She jumped to her feet, throwing herself into his waiting arms. "Oh, my God, Dad! How are you here?"

"It's a long story," he whispered into her ear, hugging her close. "I'll tell you all about it but first—" He turned to the man who'd accompanied him into the house. "Any ETA on her arrival?"

The man—a tall, sandy-haired man built like a tank—checked his watch. "Before lunch. That's all I can say for sure."

"Whose arrival?" Annie asked.

"You mother's," her father answered. "They released her from the hospital this morning and a crew of agents will be bringing her here to join us." He stroked Annie's hair. "Are you okay? I've been worried sick about you this whole time. When the men who debriefed me told me you escaped, I nearly collapsed with relief."

"I'm fine," she assured him, patting his cheek. He looked tired and too thin, older than she remembered. "How are you? You look tired."

"I am tired. And angry as hell." He kissed her forehead. "And right now, I'm a little hungry. Anything to eat in this place?"

Troy jumped in, showing them the contents of the refrigerator. Annie and her father made a couple of turkey sandwiches, while Troy heated up some canned soup, pouring the contents into a couple of mugs.

"There was a man among my captors who is apparently working for the good guys," Annie's father told her after they'd finished most of their early lunch. "He helped me escape—took a big risk to do it."

"Are you sure he was really on your side?"

"He told me his name, and when I shared it with the Cooper Security agents who met with me at the hospital, they seemed to recognize it—Damon North. Ever heard of him?"

She shook her head. "I wonder how he explained your escape?"

"He drugged the thugs who were guarding me,

so I'm not sure anyone saw him come to my rescue. Still, it was quite a chance he took."

"And you're sure you're okay?" She reached across the table and caught his hand, a little alarmed when his fingers trembled beneath hers.

"I'm sure." He squeezed her fingers. "Just need some groceries and a little shut-eye. Doctors looked me over this morning before letting me go. Just told me to eat, sleep and avoid any more kidnappings."

"Heads up," Delilah said from her spot at the patio door.

"Mother's here?" Annie asked, pushing to her feet and heading for the door.

Troy stopped her before she got there. "You need to stay away from doors and windows, Ms. Harlowe."

She frowned at him but retreated back to the table. "I hate being under lock and key. It's too much like being held captive."

"Not anywhere near the same," her father chided gently. He smiled placidly, but she saw a hint of impatience in his expression, and his gaze kept wandering over to the patio door.

It opened, finally, admitting another pair of agents and Annie's pale-faced mother, who caught sight of her daughter and husband the second she stepped foot into the door. She pushed past the guards who had helped her up the stairs and hurried into her family's embrace.

An hour later, Annie was finally satisfied that her parents were both going to be okay, despite the obvious trauma of their recent captivity. Her mother's memory problems were mostly gone, except for a blank space that seemed to cover most of her time in captivity. From her mother's description of what she could remember, it seemed clear that she'd been kept drugged most of the time, just as Wade had speculated.

"She didn't have much to offer except for leverage," Annie's father told her later, after they'd coaxed her mother into taking a nap. She was still a little weak and could clearly use the rest.

"What did you tell your captors?" Annie asked.

"More than I like to think about," her father admitted. "I told them about the coded journal."

Annie nodded, remembering what Wade had told her about the attempts to steal the journal from the Ross's house on Nightshade Island. "But not the code itself?"

He shook his head. "I couldn't allow myself to do that."

"Neither could I."

The general wrapped his arm around her. "That's why I trusted you with it, you know. Because I knew you'd protect it at all costs."

She felt his arm trembling where he held her. "Dad, why don't you lie down with Mom for a while? You could both use some sleep, and I know she'll sleep better if you're in there with her."

Her father smiled. "You're just trying to get your old man to rest."

"Guilty as charged," she said with an answering grin. "In fact, a nap sounds pretty good to me, too." She'd had little sleep over the past twenty-four hours, and it was sapping her energy as well.

"Okay." Her father cradled her face between his hands, searching her features as if he wanted to memorize them. "Just promise me you'll be here when I wake up."

"I promise."

He kissed her forehead again and opened the door to the bedroom where her mother was sleeping, closing it behind him.

With a weary sigh, Annie bypassed her own bedroom and went back into the kitchen, where four of the six bodyguards were eating a quick lunch. The other two, she saw, were moving slowly around the house, watching the perimeter for any sign of intruders.

Annie found Troy watching the street in front of the house, his posture straight and on alert. She hated to interrupt, but of the guards watching over them, he was the most likely to be able to answer her question.

"Have you heard anything from Wade?" she

asked. "Last I heard from him, he was going to confront the intruders at the security company."

Troy glanced at her, his expression mildly curious. "The intruders had fled by the time anyone got there," he said. "Wade's fine."

She frowned. So why hadn't he at least called her to let her know he was okay? Why had he let Cooper Security agents spirit her away to this safe house without even saying goodbye?

She rubbed her gritty eyes and wandered back to the bedroom she'd been assigned, settling onto the soft mattress without bothering to pull back the sheets. The tension in her back eased a little as she forced herself to relax, but the twisting sensation in the pit of her stomach remained, keeping her awake and staring at the ceiling overhead.

Had she read too much into the closeness she and Wade had begun to share? He'd admitted he didn't see himself as much of a good bet for a relationship. Maybe he thought he was sparing her heartache in the long run.

If the pain in the center of her chest meant anything, he had spared her nothing.

"THEY'VE ALL ARRIVED SAFELY." Jesse hung up the phone and looked at his brothers and sisters, who'd gathered in his office to await word on the transfer of the Harlowes to the Birmingham safe house.

Wade felt a ripple of relief dart through him,

tempered a bit by the low simmer of anger that had begun to build in his gut ever since he realized his brother had spirited Annie away from Gossamer Ridge without even giving him a chance to say goodbye.

What must she be thinking? Did she think he didn't even care enough to tell her he was okay?

"Shannon, I'd like you and Gideon to head to Birmingham as soon as possible. I want you to debrief General Harlowe about the code and how it relates to the journal we have in our possession. Specifically, I want you to find out if General Harlowe has any idea if General Ross entrusted his part of the code to anyone else. Gideon, you knew General Ross very well—maybe between yourself and General Harlowe, you can figure something out."

"Will do," Gideon agreed. He caught Shannon's hand and they left the office immediately.

"I'm going to assign a few more guards to rotate in and out with the crew currently there at the safe house," Jesse added to the others. "Meanwhile, the rest of you are going to have to work extra hours trying to figure out where our security systems failed and what we can do to shore them up." Jesse gave a dismissive nod, and the others started to disperse immediately.

Wade stuck around until the others had left. "You could have let me at least have a moment to say goodbye to Annie," he said with no preamble.

Jesse's gaze narrowed slightly. "We needed to move them immediately."

"So I'm just supposed to accept that? She's out of reach, off-limits? Would you have accepted that ten years ago if someone had tried to rip you away from Rita Marsh?"

"Someone did," Jesse snapped, his dark eyebrows arching. "Rita did. And no. I didn't take it well."

"I think I love her," Wade blurted, before he even realized what he was going to say.

Jesse fell silent for a long moment, just staring at his brother as if Wade had spoken a foreign language. "In just a few days?" he asked finally.

Wade shrugged. "I know it sounds crazy."

"You always were impulsive," Jesse murmured.

"I need to talk to her, at least. To let her know I didn't just turn my back on her."

"Can you keep your head around her?"

Wade wasn't sure how to answer. "I don't know if I can keep my head around her, but I'd take a dozen bullets for her. Does that count?"

Jesse's lips curved in a reluctant smile. "I guess it does."

"So I can go see her?"

Jesse didn't answer, watching Wade through narrowed eyes. As the silence stretched to the snapping point, Wade moved restlessly in his chair.

"Yes or no?" he asked aloud.

"Get packed. You've got bodyguard duty at the safe house."

With a grin, Wade jumped up and headed for the exit.

ANNIE MANAGED TO DOZE, if fitfully, her slumber disturbed by dark and twisted dreams of captivity and pursuit. Sometimes she was racing up an interminable number of stairs, darkness and death snapping at her heels, with nothing but infinity rising above her, no end in sight. At other times, she was back in the dark, dank hovel where her captors had imprisoned her, her legs and arms shackled in place, the future spreading endlessly, bleakly in front of her. And always, always, she was alone.

The sound of voices outside her bedroom woke her for good. She went into the bathroom and splashed some water on her face, trying not to dwell on the haggard expression staring back at her in the mirror. So much for a refreshing nap, she thought with a grimace.

She should be happy. Her parents were alive and well. They were back together, safe under the watchful eyes of a half dozen trained security agents. She had a lot to be thankful for.

*But Wade's not here,* a small voice whispered in her mind.

She felt incomplete without him here. Something vital was missing, a piece of herself that couldn't be replaced. It was crazy to feel that way, she knew, especially after only a few, short days of forced intimacy.

But just because it was crazy didn't mean it wasn't also true.

The voices came closer. A woman's voice that sounded familiar—one of Wade's sisters, Annie realized. Not Isabel or the redhead Megan. The youngest one, maybe. What was her name—Shannon?

A deeper voice answered Shannon, just outside Annie's door. Something about a journal.

General Ross's journal?

There was a soft knock on a nearby door, and Annie's father's gravelly voice greeted the newcomers. The voices drifted away, leaving the hallway silent again.

She sat on her bed again, leaning back against the headboard. Should she try to find out what Shannon Cooper and her deep-voiced friend wanted from her father? Clearly, it had something to do with General Ross's journal, and as she knew her father's part of the code as well as he did—

A knock on her bedroom door rattled her nerves. She straightened her clothes and called out, "Come in."

She'd expected Troy or one of the other bodyguards to walk into the bedroom. Anyone but Wade Cooper.

She stared at him a moment, wondering if she'd fallen asleep and started dreaming again. "Wade?"

He grinned. "I promised to let you know I made it back safely. So, I made it back safely."

She didn't know what to say. Before, when she'd thought she'd never see him again, her mind had reeled with the things she'd wanted to say to him, things she thought she'd never get the chance to express.

But now that he was here, she couldn't seem to find a word to say.

"As it turned out, the bad guys bugged out before we could get back to them," he said with a faint smile, walking slowly to her bedside. He sat on the edge, close enough to touch. But neither of them made a move toward each other.

"So I heard."

He cocked his head. "You get any sleep?"

"Not much," she admitted. Her fingers itched to touch his face, to smooth away the worry lines in his forehead. "You look tired."

"I could use a nap myself," he admitted. "By the way, I'm so happy you have your mom and dad back with you. I bet you're feeling pretty great about now."

"Of course," she agreed, forcing a smile.

His brow furrowed. "What's wrong?"

"Just some bad dreams," she said, frustrated by how he continued keeping his hands to himself. Was he trying to distance himself from her? Was this his way of telling her that the interlude between them was over?

She forced her voice past the lump in her throat. "You came all the way here just to tell me you were okay?"

"I did promise," he said with a smile.

She forced a smile of her own. "When do you have to leave?"

"Well, that's the other reason I'm here." His smile widened. "I've been assigned to guard duty here."

A flutter of excitement raced through her chest. "How long?"

"However long you're here," he answered, his smile fading. "If that's good with you."

"It's great with me," she blurted.

He moved, finally, cradling her face between his hands. "I was hoping you'd say that."

She clutched his hands. "I was so afraid I'd never see you again." She felt tears burning her eyes and blinked hard, trying to keep them from falling.

He ran his thumb lightly over her bottom lip. "I know this has all happened so quickly. Probably too quickly—"

"I just know I'm not ready to let you walk out of

my life," she said more firmly, the expression in his eyes giving her confidence. "Are you ready to walk out of mine?"

He shook his head. "No, I'm not. It's just—it's so fast. A week ago, we didn't even know each other."

"I know it's fast. And probably crazy." She slid her hands up his chest. "But I've never felt anything like this before. Not with any other man. And I don't think I can just throw it away because it's not meeting some sort of arbitrary rule about how long it's supposed to take to form a lasting attachment."

"Rebel," he murmured with a grin.

"I'm not, really, you know." She pressed her cheek against his chest, listening to the steady cadence of his heartbeat. "I'm usually very cautious about these things."

"I just don't want you to regret making a rash decision."

She looked up at his serious expression. "Who knows how long you'll be guarding me and my family? It'll certainly give us time to be sure this is what we really want. How's that for rational reasoning?"

He threaded his fingers through her hair. "Not bad, actually."

She pressed her mouth against his, her fingers curling in his T-shirt, pulling him closer. He kissed her back, a slow, maddeningly thorough exploration that made her limbs tremble and her head spin.

He snaked his arms around her waist, tugging her flush against his body until she felt as if she were melting into him.

A knock on the door interrupted just as he was pulling her down to the bed beside him. He gave a low, guttural groan. "Damn it."

"Wade?" It was Troy Cooper.

Wade pushed himself off the bed and went to the door. "Yeah?"

"Jesse's on the phone for you."

Wade looked back at Annie, his expression reluctant. She smiled at him. "Go ahead. We have time."

He grinned at her and slipped out of the door.

Annie leaned back against the pillows, smiling at the ceiling. Amazing, she thought, how radically her mood had changed since Wade Cooper walked back into her life. She'd told him they had time. But she realized, as she waited impatiently for his return, that she didn't need any more time.

Wade Cooper was the man for her. And she'd wait as long as it took to convince him she was the woman for him as well.

She just hoped it wouldn't take him too long to come to that conclusion.

WADE SLIPPED BACK INTO the bedroom without knocking and found Annie staring up at the ceiling, a faint smile on her face. She turned her head at the sound of his entrance, the smile spreading across her face like sunshine. "Everything okay?"

"So far so good," he answered, remembering Jesse's terse message over the phone. "Jesse did a little looking into that group you told us about—the Espera Group."

"Yeah?" She pushed herself into a sitting position, curiosity tempering her smile. "Did he learn anything new?"

"Maybe. Apparently they're behind a big lobbying effort going on in Congress right now, to get Congress to sign on to a treaty that limits the ability of oil-producing nations to monopolize the market. The way it's worded, it sounds pretty tempting—fairness and energy independence and all that—"

"But it's just trading one controlling force for another," Annie answered bleakly. "Do the lobbyists have the votes?"

"Not yet. But the Espera Group appears to have someone pulling strings from the inside. We just don't know who yet."

"The architect," she murmured.

He cocked his head. "Yeah?"

"Yeah. And that's not good."

"No, it's not. Jesse agrees with you—the Espera Group's agenda is too murky and dangerous to be good news. And if your father and the other two generals were right about the conspiracy—"

"Yeah." Annie's expression went grim. "But we first have to prove it."

"Well, we have the journal, and apparently Shannon and Gideon have already gotten your father to agree to help them decode the thing. From what your father says, there were things each of them kept secret, so that no one person could spill everything they knew. So we definitely have to get our hands on General Ross's part of the code."

"And General Marsh's," Annie added.

"Yeah," Wade agreed, remembering his brother's final words. "Jesse has a few ideas how to make that happen."

"We have to stop the Espera Group from getting its way."

Wade caught her hands in his. "We will."

She kissed his knuckles, smiling up at him. "I missed you."

He smiled back. "I was gone maybe five minutes."

She shrugged. "Long enough."

He settled on the bed beside her, pulling her into his embrace. She rested her cheek against his chest, her fingers playing in the fabric of his T-shirt. "You're going to be sick of having me around before this is all over."

"Don't think so." The words came out in a long yawn.

"You need a longer nap," he suggested.

She rubbed her cheek against his chest. "Will you stay here with me?"

"Sure." He cuddled her closer, stroking her cheek until her eyes drifted shut and her breathing grew slow and even. He kissed her brow. "You're stuck with me, baby," he whispered.

In her sleep, her lips curved in a smile.

\* \* \* \* \*

*Don't miss the heart-stopping conclusion of award-winning author Paula Graves's miniseries* COOPER SECURITY. *Look for* SECRET INTENTIONS *next month wherever Harlequin Intrigue books are sold!*

# LARGER-PRINT BOOKS!

## GET 2 FREE LARGER-PRINT NOVELS PLUS
## 2 FREE GIFTS!

**Harlequin**

# INTRIGUE

## BREATHTAKING ROMANTIC SUSPENSE

**YES!** Please send me 2 FREE LARGER-PRINT Harlequin Intrigue® novels and my 2 FREE gifts (gifts are worth about $10). After receiving them, if I don't wish to receive any more books, I can return the shipping statement marked "cancel." If I don't cancel, I will receive 6 brand-new novels every month and be billed just $5.24 per book in the U.S. or $5.99 per book in Canada. That's a saving of at least 13% off the cover price! It's quite a bargain! Shipping and handling is just 50¢ per book in the U.S. and 75¢ per book in Canada.* I understand that accepting the 2 free books and gifts places me under no obligation to buy anything. I can always return a shipment and cancel at any time. Even if I never buy another book, the two free books and gifts are mine to keep forever.

199/399 HDN FERE

Name _____ (PLEASE PRINT) _____

Address _____ Apt. # _____

City _____ State/Prov. _____ Zip/Postal Code _____

Signature (if under 18, a parent or guardian must sign) _____

Mail to the **Reader Service:**
**IN U.S.A.:** P.O. Box 1867, Buffalo, NY 14240-1867
**IN CANADA:** P.O. Box 609, Fort Erie, Ontario L2A 5X3
Not valid for current subscribers to Harlequin Intrigue Larger-Print books.

**Are you a subscriber to Harlequin Intrigue books
and want to receive the larger-print edition?
Call 1-800-873-8635 today or visit www.ReaderService.com.**

* Terms and prices subject to change without notice. Prices do not include applicable taxes. Sales tax applicable in N.Y. Canadian residents will be charged applicable taxes. Offer not valid in Quebec. This offer is limited to one order per household. All orders subject to credit approval. Credit or debit balances in a customer's account(s) may be offset by any other outstanding balance owed by or to the customer. Please allow 4 to 6 weeks for delivery. Offer available while quantities last.

**Your Privacy**—The Reader Service is committed to protecting your privacy. Our Privacy Policy is available online at www.ReaderService.com or upon request from the Reader Service.

We make a portion of our mailing list available to reputable third parties that offer products we believe may interest you. If you prefer that we not exchange your name with third parties, or if you wish to clarify or modify your communication preferences, please visit us at www.ReaderService.com/consumerschoice or write to us at Reader Service Preference Service, P.O. Box 9062, Buffalo, NY 14269. Include your complete name and address.